FRONTIER REVENGE

Thomas stood in his stirrups and raised his fist over his head. In a voice that must have carried out onto the prairie he shouted, "This town has killed the last of mine. I swear by Almighty God, I am going to kill this town!"

I stared at the fire in Thomas's eyes. I said, "There's a passage in the Bible, Thomas: 'Vengeance is mine, saith the lord.' "

He shook his head.

"No. This time, it's *mine*."

OTHER BOOKS BY ELMER KELTON

After the Bugles
Bowie's Mine
Captain's Rangers
Hanging Judge
Horsehead Crossing
Llano River
Manhunters
Massacre at Goliad
Stand Proud
Wagontongue
The Wolf and the Buffalo

Eyes of the Hawk

Elmer Kelton
writing as
Lee McElroy

BANTAM BOOKS

TORONTO · NEW YORK · LONDON · SYDNEY · AUCKLAND

All of the characters in this book are fictitious, and any resemblance to actual persons, living or dead, is purely coincidental.

This low-priced Bantam Book
has been completely reset in a type face
designed for easy reading, and was printed
from new plates. It contains the complete
text of the original hard-cover edition.
NOT ONE WORD HAS BEEN OMITTED.

EYES OF THE HAWK

A Bantam Book / published by arrangement with
Doubleday & Company, Inc.

PRINTING HISTORY

Doubleday edition published September 1981

Bantam edition / August 1983
2nd printing . . . . February 1986

ISBN 0-553-25651-3

Published simultaneously in the United States and Canada

Bantam Books are published by Bantam Books, Inc. Its trademark,
consisting of the words "Bantam Books" and the portrayal of a
rooster, is Registered in U.S. Patent and Trademark Office and in
other countries. Marca Registrada. Bantam Books, Inc., 666 Fifth
Avenue, New York, New York 10103.

PRINTED IN THE UNITED STATES OF AMERICA

O   11   10   9   8   7   6   5   4   3   2

Eyes of the Hawk

CHAPTER 1

No one wants you to tamper with a legend, especially by telling the truth. Over the years I have often been asked what I know of the Texas legend of Stonehill town, and of the man the Mexicans came to call the Hawk, the man who killed that town in vengeance.

I have found it convenient to live with the legend, for that is what people want to hear. The legend is mostly true, as far as it goes. But recently, feeling the growing weight of my years and knowing I may soon be learning the answers to other great mysteries, I have felt some need to set down the rest of the story as I know it. The truth will do no great injury to the legend, for the legend has a life of its own and will outlive both the truth and the teller.

Though I have lived out my graying years near what little remains of old Stonehill town, I do not often go there. Walking in the grass where her streets used to be, I can hear the wind whisper secrets through the sagging buildings that time has not yet crushed, and I imagine I hear ghosts of the years long gone rustling through her ruins. A chill comes upon me yet when I stand at the spot where *he* sat on his horse, looking down upon a boy who lay there in silence. I can see him shaking his fist in a black anger and shouting to all who could hear him that he would kill Stonehill town as mercilessly as it had murdered his son.

I prefer to remember Stonehill as I first saw it, the great freight wagons and the lumbering Mexican oxcarts challenging one another for space in the narrow streets, the busy clamor of a vital people searching for glory and riches that existed only in their dreams. They lived in hardship and squalor, and sometimes they died in a hostile wilderness, alone and afraid. But the leaders of the country told them this was necessary to the fulfillment of their manifest destiny. They accepted it, most of them, and never turned back. Good men, bad men, and those in between, they differed in many ways. But in one respect they were mostly much alike. They were people of ambition and nerve, and hunger.

I well remember my first meeting with Thomas Canfield in the old port town of Indianola. You won't find the place on a map; it was destroyed in later years by one of those killer hurricanes that occasionally roars in from the Gulf of Mexico to erase all trace of man and his works.

It was only a small town with perhaps one or two permanent stone buildings when I landed there off of the merchant vessel *James Callahan* in the winter of 1854–55. I was the youngest of several sons on a small cotton farm along the Mississippi delta in Louisiana. My parents were too poor to have slaves, so they had children instead. My limited schooling gave me enough skill with ciphers to understand that my share of the family holdings would not long shield me from starvation once I left the protective roof. At seventeen I put all my personal belongings upon my back, hired as a crewman on a boat hauling a load of cotton, and shortly found myself exploring the wonders of New Orleans. I found much there to interest and no little to tempt a boy whose pockets are empty, as mine soon were. I further discovered that few people would hire even a strong and willing white boy for wages when they had slaves to do the heavy lifting without pay. I also found people in general agreement that Texas was a wondrous land where money lay in the streets, just waiting for someone to pick it up. At first opportunity I hired as a laborer on the *James Callahan,* which was hauling manufactured goods to Texas and would be bringing cotton back.

It did not take me long to decide that a seaman's life was not cut to my frame, for I spent more time at the rail than at my work. The captain probably would have fired me had we not already passed over the bar and were well out to sea. Once the sickness passed, he saw to it that I made up for the lost time. It was, all in all, a miserable passage. We ran into one major winter storm that brought me fear of a type I had never known; I was certain I would soon drown in that cold, terrible water. But I was not so lucky, for all I did was become deathly ill from an attack of the grippe, brought on by working on deck soaked to the skin. I wished mightily that I could die and end the misery. But my protecting angel had remained in New Orleans.

Even at the beginning I had intended to remain a sailor only long enough to reach Texas, and my experiences on shipboard only served to deepen my resolve in this direction. I felt duty-bound to remain with the crew long enough to see the cargo unloaded, but I felt no such duty toward seeing the waiting cotton bales carried aboard. I took my pay from the captain's reluctant hands and quickly found how meager it was when I tried to convert it into the necessities of life ashore. It took much less time to spend than to earn.

Indianola offered no employment to such as I, and no money was lying in the streets. If there had ever been, the constant stream of humanity passing through had picked it up and made off with it long before I had my chance. I decided the fortune, if there was one, must lie somewhere inland.

I ate little and slept beneath a wharf while awaiting my chance. Even for a boy whose main concern was a hungry belly, there was much to marvel over. It was my first time to see the big Mexican oxcarts, their wooden wheels as high as a man's shoulder. The axles were crude and squealed in pain when not well greased, so that the carts' coming was known before they broke into view. The Mexicans themselves were a cu-

riosity to me—little men, most of them, rattling away in a foreign tongue that made no sense in my ear. I had heard Cajun
French, but I could find no similarity between that and the
quick-fire Spanish these people spoke. I was fascinated by their
wide *sombreros,* by the great jingling spurs worn by the
horsemen.

I had heard, of course, about the two wars the Texans had
fought against Mexico, and I had assumed those were long
since over. They were not, except in name. The Texas freight
wagons came lumbering into town, many hauling bales of cotton and general farm produce to be shipped back to the other
states for money. I sensed the enmity which flared between
these people and the little men of the brown-leather skin.
Around the wharf I heard casual talk about a "cart war," a rivalry between the Mexican cartmen and the *gringo* wagoners
over the freight business between the ports and inland markets
such as San Antonio. I heard it said that many men had died or
disappeared on those long, dusty trails that wound through the
brush country, men of both persuasions.

On my second day I saw a Mexican and a Texan meet with
knives in hand after a wagon and a cart hung wheels on an Indianola street. Nobody in the crowd moved to stop the fight
until it became clear the Mexican was about to win. Then a
broad-shouldered Texan with red beard and long rusty-colored
hair swung a singletree and clubbed the Mexican to the ground.
I was satisfied the cart driver was dead, but friends carried him
away. Later I saw the little man sitting up beside a campfire, his
head swathed in dirty bandages. I decided they were a hardy
lot, these Texas people, whether light-skinned or dark.

On inquiry I found that the red-bearded man was named
Branch Isom. He bossed a string of wagons that was loading
goods I had helped carry off of the *James Callahan.* It was said
he would be taking them to San Antonio by way of Stonehill. I
had never heard of Stonehill, and San Antonio sounded considerably more romantic. Perhaps it was there that money lay in

the streets. I went to his camp and found him sitting on a bed-roll, leaning his back against the huge rear wheel of a freight wagon. He held a cup of coffee in one hand and an open whisky bottle in the other, taking a sip of each in its own turn. A coldness in his eyes made me hesitate in my last steps.

I said, "Mr. Isom, I am Reed Sawyer."

No change came in his eyes. He studied me in cold silence, then asked, "Is there any reason that should be of interest to me?"

"I would like a job with your wagons to San Antonio."

He scowled. "I suppose you'd expect to be paid for it."

"Only what is customary. I was paid fifty cents a day, meals and a bunk on the ship. With your wagons there would be only the meals."

His voice was as cold as his eyes. "You don't look healthy to me. You've probably got some disease you'd spread to every-body in the crew."

"I had the grippe on board. I am over that now. I am strong. I can do my share of the work."

He laughed, but it was not the kind of warm, friendly laugh you like to hear. "There are people in this port who would pay *me* to take them along, and they'd work for nothing. Why should I pay *you*? Get away from here, boy, before I sic my dogs on you."

I saw the dogs, big ugly gray brutes of uncertain ancestry. They looked as if they would chew a man's legs off on com-mand. A chill ran up my back. I turned without saying more and walked away from Isom's camp. The smell of the coffee and the cooking food went with me, for I had not eaten all day. I bought a fish from a man on the beach, roasted it over an open fire, then slept in my accustomed damp place beneath the wharf.

It was the next morning that the Polanders arrived. They came up the trail from Galveston. I learned later that they had been with a larger group of mixed Europeans who had landed there but had been delayed in Galveston by fever, so that the main body went ahead without them. Now, after having buried one or two of their party they had come on, bound for a settlement already laid out for them many days' journey inland.

They seemed as strange to me in their own way as the Mexicans. Having had little time for the study of geography, I had only the vaguest knowledge of the various European countries' names, much less their locations. For all I knew, Poland was a part of Africa. Mostly I looked at the women, particularly the young ones. At seventeen, I found it particularly interesting that they wore the shortest skirts I had seen except in the drinking halls of New Orleans. The skirts ended above the ankles, a scandalous sight. The better people of Indianola were quick to decide that these were loose women, for only that sort would flaunt themselves so. Some of the immigrant women wore wooden shoes, and most had black felt hats with wide brims.

People were laughing and pointing, but somehow I was stirred to pity, not laughter. These immigrants looked as hungry and poor as I was myself. At least I had the advantage of being able to speak with the people around me. These Polanders talked in a tongue that no one in Indianola seemed able to understand. They tried making signs but had scant success even with that. I could only imagine how they had made themselves understood well enough in Galveston that they hired Mexican cartmen to haul their belongings. In four big two-wheeled carts were piled trunks and a few featherbeds and some wooden farm implements they had brought from the old country.

Branch Isom came along to watch the show, he and some of his wagon men. It was obvious he had little regard for the foreigners. He had even less when he saw they were using Mexican cartmen. "Birds of a feather," he grumbled. "Dumb heathens, there's not one of them that understands English."

A man at his side said, "I wonder if they understand *dog*."

Those ugly gray curs had followed. The man sicced them onto the oxen that pulled the lead cart. Trapped in crude and heavy wooden yokes, the poor brutes kicked at the dogs and then tried to run. They only succeeded in dragging the cart into a ditch. It tipped over, spilling trunks and wooden plows and bedding onto the ground. The strange-looking foreigners went running after, trying to spare their goods further damage. They chunked rocks at the dogs and whipped them with sticks until the pair gave up and retreated to their master.

It was then that Thomas Canfield rode up. He seemed to appear from nowhere, sitting on a long-legged, beautifully built sorrel horse in the middle of the street. He was a tall man, not blocky and stout like Isom but well built just the same. He was then only in his early twenties but already mature in features, his bearing proud. He was clearly a man sure where he was going and unwilling to waste time along the way.

He said sternly, "Isom, do you want to talk some business, or had you rather bedevil a bunch of poor foreigners who have already had hell enough?"

Isom turned. His manner showed that this man on horseback was one he respected, though I also got the idea he did not particularly like him. "Hello, Canfield. What business could I possibly have with you?"

"That depends on how willing you are to talk price. Some goods came for me on that last ship out of New Orleans. I want them hauled to Stonehill."

The dogs stood by Isom's legs, their tongues hanging out. They still looked toward the ditched cart, considering the peril of renewed assault. One of them decided to try and started back toward the cart. Isom said sharply, "Here, dogs! Stay here." They obeyed. Isom had a voice that commanded obedience of man or beast. "What kind of goods?" he asked.

Canfield said, "Farm implements."

The foreigners did not understand the talk. It came to me later, when I took time to think about it, that they thought Thomas Canfield had come to their rescue and had ordered Isom to halt the harassment. One of the young women—just a

girl, really—looked at Canfield with open admiration. In a minute Canfield caught the look, and he stared back at the girl.

Isom said, "Farm implements are heavy. I'll have to look at
the load before we can figure."

Canfield didn't hear him; he was distracted by the girl. So
was I. It was her ankles which got my attention at first. Growing up, I had had to take it on faith that girls even had ankles.
But she had a pleasant face, too, and soft brown eyes that
reminded me of a doe. Her full attention was devoted to
Canfield, and his to her.

Isom repeated himself. Canfield nodded. They started together toward the wharf, Canfield still riding that big sorrel,
Isom walking with the dogs behind him.

None of the American people helped the foreigners get the
cart out of the ditch. Most simply went on about their business.
In a few minutes some Mexican cartmen came along, and the
Mexicans who were with the Polanders called on them for help.
They had to finish unloading the heavy goods out of the cart. In
a bit they manuevered the oxen up and got the big wooden
wheels back on flat ground. Then all of the Polanders, women
as well as the men, set in to loading their goods back into place.
I stayed out of it at first because I didn't figure it was any of my
business, but then I started thinking that if I helped I might be
invited to share a meal with somebody. I didn't know what kind
of food Mexicans or Polanders ate, but anything was better
than fish roasted on a stick over an open fire, which was all I
had had for three days. I pitched in and helped lift the heavy
trunks and the wooden plows. Not until later did I realize I
wouldn't recognize an invitation to supper if they gave me one.
I never knew there were so many strange languages in one
place.

One thing most people don't realize is that Texas was a
mixed lot of humanity in those days. There seems to be a
mistaken impression that early Texas had just two kinds of
people: leftover Mexicans and Bible-reading, whisky-drinking,

rifle-shooting, English-speaking immigrants from Tennessee. In truth, it wasn't like that at all. Texas drew people from all over the world because it was so big, and it had so much land to offer. It was considered a place for starting anew, no matter what fate had dealt to each person before. All kinds of people moved to Texas. Wherever you went, you found settlements of Germans, Swedes, Irish, French, Czechs. It was a Babel without a tower. It was a melting pot that never quite melted.

I didn't find a soul in the party that I could talk with, so I stood off to one side, looking hungry and waiting to see what might happen. In a little while Thomas Canfield rode back from the wharf with a grim look on his face. I assumed Isom had asked him more than he had expected to haul his goods. Canfield headed directly up to the Polanders and spoke to the Mexican cartmen who had come along and helped reload the cart. I could tell he was struggling with the language. In later years he could talk Spanish like a native. But even when I first saw him, he was able to understand and make himself understood.

In a little he was accompanied back toward the wharf by a couple of Mexicans. Branch Isom stood in front of a dramshop watching, his face clouded and angry. When Canfield returned he was followed by two smiling Mexican freighters. Isom turned and went into the dramshop, slamming the door against the wintry chill blowing in off of the water.

Canfield rode by the Polanders, tipped his low-crowned hat and said, "Good morning." The voice was slow and Southern. The people didn't know what he said, but he spoke in a kindly way, so they smiled. Especially the girl.

I decided if he was feeling so good, it was time for me to present myself and hope for better than I had received at the hands of Branch Isom. I said, "Mister, could I talk to you?"

He glanced at me in surprise. I realized he thought I was one of the Polanders. "You speak English?" he asked.

"That's *all* I talk," I told him. "These aren't my people."

"I didn't mean to offend you. They look like a decent sort. It isn't their fault they were born somewhere else."

In those days nearly everybody in Texas except the Mexicans had been born somewhere else, but most of them not quite so far away as the Polanders.

I said, "I take it you're going inland. I was wondering if I could travel with you? I'll work at anything."

He looked me over carefully. "You have kin that you're going to?"

"I've got nobody here. I'm looking for work to do, and a place to go to away from this coast. This is a feverish country, and poor."

"Anyplace is a poor country when you've got no money. I judge you have none?"

"Very little," I admitted. "But I have a good back and willing hands."

He wanted to know where my gun was, and I told him I owned none. I couldn't tell whether that pleased him or worried him. It was a little of both, I think.

"Well," he said finally, "I can't guarantee that you'll find any work where I'm going, but you're welcome to come with me. I don't suppose you have a horse?"

I barely owned a pair of shoes.

As he rode up the street, I followed him afoot. Branch Isom stepped out of the dramshop with a bottle in his hand. His face was half as red as his hair and his beard. "Hold up, Canfield," he said.

Thomas Canfield pulled the sorrel to a stop. His manner was that of a man doing something because he chose to, not because he had been ordered to. "I don't believe we have any business, Isom."

"Yes, we do. You've hired those Mexican cartmen."

"They bid the haul for half what you asked me."

"They're Mexicans. I'm white."

"My freight has no eyes to tell the difference. But my wallet knows when I take only half as much out of it."

"You can't expect a white man to work that cheap."

I was tempted to remind Isom that he had expected me not only to work for nothing but to pay for the privilege. I held my tongue, confident that Thomas Canfield could maintain his side of the conversation. Canfield said, "The deal has been made. Next time you want to do business with me, Isom, don't try to get rich all at one time."

Isom took the advice as a challenge. "If you shipped with me, I'd guarantee protection for your goods. You ship with those Mexicans at your own risk."

"That sounds like a threat."

"No threat. I am only pointing out to you that there has been trouble on the trails. Mexican cart trains have been burned, and the shippers took a loss."

"White men's wagons have been burned too."

"Not mine. And mine are not going to be."

"Neither are my goods, Isom." His voice dropped a little, so that I strained to hear him. "I'll kill the man who tries."

He and Isom stared at each other with a look that was near hatred. Without anybody framing it in words, a challenge had been flung, and answered. Isom shrugged. "You're twenty-one."

Canfield nodded. "And a few years more."

Isom went back into the dramshop, the bottle in his hand. Canfield stared after him a moment, then turned to me as I walked up even with his horse. "You heard all that, Reed Sawyer?"

I told him I had. He said, "You may want to reconsider going with me."

"He didn't *say* he was going to do anything."

"Yes, he did. You were only listening to his words."

"I still want to go," I said. "I've been in this town long enough."

"Do you know how to use a gun?"

In truth, my poor marksmanship had been a source of shame to my father, for to most farm boys in Louisiana handling a rifle was second nature; it was a boy's job to keep meat in the house. I did not admit to my shortcoming. I said, "I grew up with a rifle in my hand."

"Then I'll provide you one."

I followed him to his camp, such as it was. He had staked a packhorse on grass at the edge of the little town. In camp waited a Mexican man several years older than Canfield. "Meet Amadeo Fernandez," Canfield said to me. I shook hands with the Mexican and said I was pleased to know him. He answered in Spanish. He smiled, so I knew at least that he was not cursing me. That was the only way I could have known the difference.

I made some comment to the effect that if I had known few people in Texas spoke English I might have chosen to go elsewhere. It was the first time I saw Canfield smile. Smiling was not a thing he did often, then or later in his life. He said, "The truth is the truth no matter what language it is spoken in. And a lie is a lie."

In the pack, spread out on the ground, was some flour for bread, some coffee beans, grease and smoked pork. I hungered for the pork, but to my chagrin Canfield did not touch it. He said, "I had Amadeo buy us some fish. It has been a long time since I have had fresh saltwater fish."

Having contributed nothing toward the meal, I could ill afford to be critical. But I ate rather more of the bread than of the fish.

I felt it was not politic to ask questions about his business. He volunteered a little information, however, as we ate. He said he owned land north and east of Stonehill. He was farming part of it, raising cattle on the rest. His parents had moved to that region soon after the Mexican War and had broken out one of the first fields. Thomas was a good farmer, but his preference lay in other directions. He had gone west into Indian country with a party of horse hunters, capturing wild mustangs to bring back to the settlements for sale and trade. With his share of the

profits he had bought the first land of his own. Later he went
back into the Comanche hunting grounds with hired Mexicans
and took more wild horses. This time the profit was his. He
added more land to his holdings.

"All kinds of people are coming into this country," he said.
"You saw those Polanders. A San Antonio priest bought property for them to break out and work, over past Stonehill. Some
of them haven't brought any equipment. There's no one to buy
it from where they're going, no one but me. I've been ordering
farm implements shipped from New Orleans and reselling them
to new farmers. Whatever I can make, I'll put into more land."

I ventured, "You must be a big man up there."

"Not yet. But I will be."

By next morning the Mexican cartmen had enough freight to
fill out their loads. One of those big carts, drawn by two yokes
of oxen, could haul up to five thousand pounds. The four Mexicans who had been carrying goods for the Polanders joined at
the end of the line. Canfield talked worriedly in Spanish to
Amadeo Fernandez. Together they rode back to where the foreigners waited. I followed at a respectful distance and listened
to the arguments. I knew none of the language but surmised
from the hand motions that the Polanders and their Mexican
freighters intended to go along. Canfield was trying to tell them
this cart train carried special danger, but he did not convince
the four Mexicans. The Polanders listened in worried silence,
understanding neither English nor Spanish. Finally a man came
out of a warehouse and began speaking to them in still another
language, which I learned was German. A couple of the Polanders understood that fairly well. So Spanish was translated
into English through Canfield, then into German and finally,
for the good of all the group, into the Silesian dialect spoken by
the Polanders.

I could only imagine how much was lost or distorted through
all the translations.

I began to think I should give Texas just a little more of my time, and if conditions did not improve I would move on to a more promising locale where everyone spoke my language.

At the time I thought the immigrants simply did not understand the seriousness of the situation. Later I learned they had already been through so much hell that the prospect of a little more caused no terror for them.

Canfield was looking at the girl. Talking to her was hopeless, but he tried. "I wish I could make you understand. You ought not to be on this trip."

She only smiled. It was not for the women to make the decisions anyway, not in those times or among the European immigrants. Canfield had no authority over the cart train; he was simply a shipper. But he would see his goods protected. I was to learn that when he felt something belonged to him, whether people or land or cattle, he would fly into the face of the devil to protect it.

Branch Isom and his wagons were still in Indianola when the cart train pulled out onto the well-beaten road. The wagoners had not yet gotten a full load, but a merchant vessel had docked late the night before and they would probably receive enough freight from it to finish out.

Isom stood in front of the dramshop with three of his teamsters as the last of the Mexican cartmen goaded his oxen into movement with the Polanders' goods. I was still afoot, of course, but so were the other people. Even the cart drivers walked most of the time. Thomas Canfield and Fernandez were on horseback, the Mexican leading the packhorse.

I looked back at Isom and said to Canfield, "At least they will be well behind us."

Canfield shook his head. "They have mule teams, not oxen. They will catch up."

It took most of that first day to get up out of the low-lying, swampy coastal lands and onto higher, drier ground. Though it was winter, the sun was strong and the air muggy. I found myself sweating, and I feared lapsing back into the fever that had plagued me on the ship. But as we worked our way up into a drier elevation I began to feel better and take more interest in the life I saw around me. We were passing through a country already partially settled, much of the better land broken for cultivation. This was the fallow time for most of it. The farmers we saw were mostly breaking out new land to go into crops the following spring. Though the great high-wheeled carts were still a curiosity to me, I noted that the people we passed paid little or no attention to them. But the Polanders were another matter. People stared and whispered as the strange procession of immigrants passed. I knew most people were fascinated as I had been by their clothes, particularly those of the women. A boy of ten or twelve, riding bareback on a shaggy mule in the direction opposite our line of travel, watched with open mouth as the Polanders passed. He turned the mule around and whipped it into a lope back the way he had come. A mile or so down the road we passed a couple of crude farmhouses built of logs. At least a dozen people stood in front, the boy among them. They looked at the immigrants as if they had been a circus parade.

I was bringing up the rear afoot. Canfield and Fernandez had ridden up front somewhere. A couple of the farmers edged closer and closer and looked me over carefully. Finally deciding I was of another breed than the Polanders, they fell in beside me.

"What kind of queer varmints are those?" the older one asked me.

I told him I understood they were Polanders but added that I didn't rightly know what a Polander was. All I knew for certain was that they had come from the other side of the big water.

"What are they good for?" he wanted to know.

I told him I supposed they were farmers inasmuch as I had seen some wooden plows. But I hadn't been able to talk to them, so I didn't really know.

"Foreigners," he said with a snort. "Every time we look up

there's another kind of foreigners passing by. Germans, Frenchies, Sweders—God knows what all. We no sooner taken this land away from those Indians and Mexicans than all these foreigners start coming in. You watch, they'll be taking it away from *us* one of these days."

From what I had heard Texas still had more than enough land for everybody, but I judged he didn't care to hear that.

Through the day we passed other freight outfits coming from the interior, headed down to Indianola and Galveston. When they were Mexican oxcart trains there was a great deal of laughing and yelling between their men and ours. When they were American wagons, the hatred that passed from one side to the other was so thick and heavy you could almost reach out and touch it. I had never realized how long it took to get over a war, even after the battles had stopped.

Canfield said the hatred had come first, before the wars, and it would last a long time yet because people on both sides kept studying on the differences between themselves. They didn't pay much attention to the ways they were alike. Each one was convinced the other was inferior. They all talked to the same God, but they saw Him differently and were sure He was on their side alone.

All the Mexicans I had seen up to then were the ones on this train and a few in Indianola. To me they were still as strange as the Polanders. The difference in languages stood like a stone wall between us. I asked Canfield how he got along with them to the extent that he even rode with one, that he let them freight his goods for him when white men were available to do it.

"I learned a lot from Amadeo," he said. "He worked for my father, and now he works for me. Sure, some Mexicans will lie to you. So will Branch Isom. Some of them will cheat you. So will Branch Isom. Some of them will even kill you if there's a profit in it. So will Branch Isom. So where's the big difference?"

Late that evening the Mexicans reached a place they wanted

to camp. They found another cart train there ahead of them, coming down toward the coast. Both trains camped together to double their defense. I could tell there was a considerable amount of excited talk between the Mexicans of the two outfits, but of course I couldn't understand a word of it. As we fixed ourselves a little supper out of the goods in Canfield's pack he told me there was talk of a cart train being raided a couple of days' journey ahead. The attack had been driven off, but there had been some loss of life and a couple of carts burned.

Attempted robbery was the reason which went down in official records, but the cartmen knew robbery was no issue. This was part of a sustained warfare between Mexican and American freighters for supremacy on the trail. Many San Antonio merchants favored the Mexicans because they charged less for making the haul. The Mexicans had less investment in equipment and were willing to live by lower standards. Americans needed more money because of their higher investments and their higher expectations. The issues were simple. Only the solution was difficult. Canfield said he expected the outcome would be decided more on the basis of force than of equity.

In the long run, he added, most conflicts are.

We were under no obligation to help the cartmen stand guard, and it was clear that those of the coast-bound train did not trust Canfield or me. One of the first Mexican words I learned to recognize was *gringo*, spoken like a curse. But Canfield and I each took a turn anyway, with Amadeo filling out the last part of the night. Nothing happened except a fight between Canfield's horse and one of the others. The sorrel quickly established dominance.

We were on the trail soon after sunup, the great carts creaking and squealing. A couple of the Polanders seemed to have trouble getting started. A woman of middle age was supported by younger women until a teamster made motions for her to be placed in a cart, where she could ride. I gathered that she had survived the fever—a common complaint along the coast—and she had not yet regained her strength. Canfield rode to the cart and helped lift the woman into it. He received a smile from the pretty girl for his efforts. I suspected that had been his object in the first place.

One of the cartmen had a lean brown dog. As the day wore on, the dog spent most of its time with the Polanders, who talked to him in their strange language and patted him on the head. He wagged his tail and seemed to understand them perfectly well.

I brought up the rear, carrying a long-barreled muzzle-loading rifle Canfield had lent me. Toward noon I began hearing a racket behind us and saw a wagon train gradually catching up. A horseman rode well out in front of it. As he neared I recognized Branch Isom's red beard, and the two bad dogs trailing along on either side of him. We pulled off the trail for nooning, and Isom brought his wagons past. He looked us over with hard eyes and said nothing. Not a word was spoken by anyone on either his train or ours. The only communication was between Isom's two dogs and the brown one which belonged to our train. They had a snarling match that led to a moment of tooth-snapping conflict. Isom rode back and popped a whip over the dogs' heads. His two pulled out of the fight and followed him, though they looked back and continued the quarrel so long as they were within range.

One of the cartmen patted the brown dog and spoke approvingly for his bravery in battle. He would have lost if the fight had been allowed to go on much longer, but it would have been to superior numbers, not to superior gallantry. The pretty immigrant girl got something out of a cart and smeared it on the dog's wounds, talking softly in words the dog seemed to understand even though I did not.

While we rested, one of the immigrant men came to me and began talking. He pointed to my rifle and made motions I could not decipher until finally he mimed the act of pulling a bowstring. I realized he was asking if there was a chance we might encounter Indians. I didn't know.

Canfield said, "No Indians. They're a long way west." Evidently his meaning was understood, for the Polander seemed relieved.

I said, "These people are in for a lot of trouble if they've got to go through this every time they want to talk to anybody."

Canfield said, "They'll get with their own and stay with their own. There'll be a few who will learn enough English to get by, and those will take care of the rest. I've sold plows to some Germans, and that's the way they've done it. These immigrants don't scatter amongst us much; they stay close together and lean on one another. They'll make it."

Watching these people, the language difference a barrier between us, I could only guess at what they had left behind them, what they had been through to get here. Later, when the barriers began to break down, I would learn that the Polanders were something like the Israelites of the Bible, made slaves in their own country and finally driven out. They had been conquered and divided up by the Prussians and others and their lands had been taken away from them until they faced the proposition of leaving or starving. There had been a few Polanders in Texas at the time of the revolution from Mexico, and some had been executed on Santa Anna's orders after the fight at Goliad. A few were with Sam Houston when he won the battle of San Jacinto. These wrote letters home, and so over the next few years they kept drawing in friends and family until they had several small communities spread across the country. The stories about money lying in the streets had probably reached Silesia too, just as they had reached Louisiana.

I doubted they were any more disappointed than I was to find out how little money existed in Texas, and none of it lying in the streets. They had chosen a hard time to come. Actually, it was always hard times in Texas. The rich you could count on one hand. The poor you found in multitudes.

Late in the day the Mexicans began stepping out of the trail
and looking forward. The *capitán* rode back and visited with
Amadeo, then the two spurred their horses and rode far out
ahead, beyond sight. A while before dark they were back, disappointed. Canfield said they had hoped to meet another cart
train coming down the trail so they could camp together for
mutual protection, but they had found none. Now they could
not put off camping any longer; it would soon be night.

The Polanders would probably have helped with guard duty
if they had been asked, but no one knew how to ask them. So
far as we could tell, they had not a single weapon with them.
They had not been accustomed to owning or using them in the
old country; the Prussians would not have allowed it. We two
gringos and the Mexicans divided the guard duty between us. I
had not thought about it until Canfield mentioned it, for I was
not used to having to consider such things, but the *capitán* had
camped the train in a broad, open area. If the moon was again
bright and cold as the night before, we would have good visi-
bility.

Because I could talk to no one else, I took Canfield as my
example and copied whatever he did. He was concerned but not
really fearful. I could not say the same for myself. I had never
held a gun in my hands for possible use against another human.
I asked, "Do you have to do this all the time?" It crossed my
mind that I was still only two days' walk from the coast.

Canfield said, "When I was a boy we saw a few Indians, but
they've all been pushed west. Once we're home nobody will
bother us. But the trail is always a place to be watchful. Especially as long as this cart war goes on."

It seemed to me it would have been the better part of valor
to have shipped his goods with Isom or some other wagon man
no matter what the rate had been. I said as much.

Canfield told me sternly, "In this country you must never
show a feather. Give up to them once and you're beaten."
Through the years to come I was to learn just how deeply he

believed that. Once challenged, cost was no factor to him. He never showed a feather.

The night chill closed upon us as soon as the sun dropped out of sight. When the people spread their blankets to sleep, one of the immigrants threw fresh wood upon their campfire. Canfield quickly dragged it back out of the flames. He tried to explain that for safety's sake it was better to keep a dark camp. I don't think he quite conveyed the message, but he had such a commanding way about him that no one presented any challenge.

I took the first watch. I doubted I could have slept anyway. Thomas Canfield seemed able to command himself even in the matter of sleeping, for within a few minutes after he rolled up in his blankets he was gone. It took Amadeo Fernandez a bit longer. I sat hunched with my coat on and my blanket wrapped around my shoulders, my bare hands stiff and cold on the steel barrel of the rifle. There was no danger of my falling asleep on duty. I was chilled to the bone.

I had no way of telling time and had not learned to follow the stars. I listened for the Mexicans who stood watch farther up the line of carts. When at last I heard them changing guard, I got up, trembling from the cold, and carefully awakened Canfield. He wasted no time yawning. He seemed to know where he was and what he had to do from the moment he opened his eyes. He got up and went about it in a quiet, businesslike manner. I lay down on the spot he had vacated, hoping he had warmed the ground. He had not. I shivered a long time before I dropped off to sleep.

When I awakened it was suddenly and to the sound of shots. I flung the blanket away and fumbled in panic for the rifle. I saw flashes of fire and vague movements out in the night. I heard men shouting and horses running. I had never realized how quickly a man could fire and then recharge a muzzle-loading rifle until I saw Thomas Canfield do it.

My heart pounded and skipped. I shouted, "What do I shoot at?"

He replied, "Anything that moves out there. We've got no friends past the cart line."

Some riders carried torches. Though they held them high, the flickering light showed the horses a little. Somewhere up the line I heard a man scream, and I saw a torch thrown into one of the carts. Behind me the immigrant women were crying, huddling together.

From out of the night a shape lunged at me, and I raised my rifle. It was close range, but I missed. Canfield was busy reloading. The horseman spurred into me, knocking me down and making me lose my hold on the rifle. The rider hurled a blazing torch into the nearest cart, one which held immigrant goods. A Polander jumped onto the cart and grabbed the torch, flinging it back into the horseman's face as the man fired a pistol. The horse squealed in panic at the blaze and whirled around while the man cursed. Canfield finished loading his rifle, brought it to his shoulder and fired. The man was driven back in his saddle. The horse broke into a run. The rider slid over its rump and landed roughly on the ground. Instantly Canfield was kneeling over him, a long hunting knife in his hand, the point pressing against the man's throat.

"You move," he said, "and I'll kill you."

The man groaned. The rifle ball had taken him hard.

Canfield glared at me as he reloaded his rifle. "I thought you said you could shoot."

I had no answer for that and did not try one.

"Watch him, then," Canfield said tersely and turned his attention back to the men out there in the moonlight. He called a time or two for Amadeo. Both of us had lost sight of the Mexican.

The shooting died. The raiders pulled back, for they had flung their torches and had found the defense too strong. Down the line, one cart blazed. Despairing of putting out the fire, several Mexicans grabbed the tongue and pulled the vehicle away from the others to prevent its fire from spreading. Canfield said with concern, "I'm going to see if that's one of the carts carrying my goods."

The wounded raider kept groaning. I did not know what to do about him, so I did nothing except watch.

One of the Polanders touched my shoulder and pointed to the other side of the carts. He said something I did not understand except that the word "Mexican" somehow came out of it. I handed another Polander my rifle and pointed to the wounded man, hoping he understood that I meant for him to stand guard. He took the weapon nervously. Following the older man's repeated beckoning, I found two of the immigrant women kneeling over a fallen Amadeo. They spoke softly, trying to comfort him. He probably did not hear them. As little experience as I had had with that sort of thing, I sensed he was dying. I touched him and felt the stickiness of warm blood and came near being sick. I brought my hand quickly away, as if I had stuck it into fire. In the excitement I had forgotten about the cold, but suddenly it came back to me, and I was trembling all over.

Canfield called me. I responded with what voice I could muster. He came around the cart, knelt quickly and called Amadeo's name. The Mexican's breathing was spaced in ragged patches, and in a few moments it stopped. Canfield talked softly in Spanish, gently shaking the man as if he thought he could force breath back into the body. Finally he pushed to his feet and walked back to where the wounded raider lay. Canfield towered over him with fury in his face.

The man pleaded, "Help me."

Canfield looked at me. "Go relight one of those torches at that cart fire and bring it here so I can see."

I did. He held the torch over the man's face. "I know you," he said accusingly. "I've seen you in Stonehill. You're with Isom's train, aren't you?"

The man cried, "I'm bleeding to death. Help me."

"Tell me first," Canfield insisted. "It was Isom who led this raid, wasn't it?"

One of the Mexican cartmen dropped to one knee to tear the clothing away from the wound deep in the raider's shoulder. Canfield pushed the man to one side. He said something in Spanish, then said for my benefit and the prisoner's, "We'll treat you when you've told me what I want to know. Till then, nobody touches you."

"I'll die," the man cried weakly.

"Then die," Canfield said. His voice was as cold as the night. "It's up to you."

He stood over the man, a terrible look on his face. I saw a ferocity I had never seen anywhere before. Slowly the Mexicans began gathering around. They talked quietly among themselves, and I heard a word that I later learned described the look they saw in his eyes: *gavilán*. The hawk.

At that moment I think Thomas Canfield might have killed anyone who had stepped in to thwart what he was doing. I suddenly found that I was a little afraid of him, a feeling I never quite lost. There was a look about him then—and I saw it again at times through the years—that turned my blood cold.

It was, for a little while, a contest of wills between Canfield and the wounded *gringo*. Finally, as it would always be, it was the other man who gave up first. He lifted his hand a little way, pleadingly, and whispered, "I'll tell. Help me."

"Tell first," Canfield said.

The man tried, but he had waited too long. The strength was gone from him, and his voice. His lips moved, but no discernible words came. Canfield knelt and grabbed the man's collar. He shook him. "Louder! Tell me! Was it Isom?"

He had won the contest, but the victory cost him a price he had not intended to pay. The man died without telling him what he wanted to know. Canfield stood over the dead raider and cursed him for taking the life of a better man.

CHAPTER 2

Dawn came and we buried the dead, but not together. Canfield would not have that. It was a custom of the time that Americans and Mexicans not be buried side by side, but this was not Canfield's reason. He said bitterly that Amadeo Fernandez was a God-fearing man too good to keep company with an outlaw throughout eternity. We buried them on opposite sides of the trail. Canfield quoted Scripture by memory. The Mexicans worried that Amadeo needed the services of a priest to keep him safe from the devil, but many a good man had been buried along this road without the benefit of clergy. The immigrants bowed their heads and offered up a prayer. I did not know if it was for Amadeo or for their own deliverance. None of them had been hurt during the shooting, and their possessions were but little damaged.

The dead *gringo* had carried little worth salvaging except for a knife and pistol, unused, and his rifle. Canfield gave me these in recognition of the fact that I owned no weapons and that henceforth I might have need for them as a result of having been in the cartmen's company. A little silver was found in the man's pockets. Canfield took this for Amadeo's widow.

I tried the accuracy of the rifle by resting its barrel in the fork of a tree and aiming at a dried cowchip forty yards away. The bullet kicked up dust short of the chip. I was satisfied that the rifle was more accurate than the man who fired it. Canfield seemed to agree, though he did not say so. The pistol was one of the cap-and-ball style of the time, heavy as a sack of lead bars. It took a while to accustom myself to wearing it, for I developed a strong list in its direction.

The outlaw's horse had gotten away, but I probably would not have had more than temporary possession had we managed to capture it. There was always somebody around to claim a horse if there seemed any doubt about its true ownership.

I was set to walk, but Canfield pointed his chin toward Amadeo's horse. "You'd just as well ride. I don't care to lead him."

The stirrups were longer than was comfortable, but I put up with the inconvenience because refitting them would take time. I had no wish to be left alone now, even for a little while. I felt nervous about riding a dead man's saddle. I asked, "Did he have a family?"

Canfield was grim. "A wife and two boys."

"What happens to them now?"

"They'll stay on my place as long as I have one, and as long as they want to." His jaw ridged. I could see vengeance in his eyes, but there was frustration too. Though he was convinced Branch Isom had been at the foot of this, he had no legal recourse. One thing I learned about Thomas Canfield as time went by was that he had two characteristics in abundance: determination and a long memory. He had also a third: an inability to forgive. Somewhere, sometime, his chance would come. He was always ready. Meantime, he could wait.

A change came over the people on the cart train. Quietly, without anyone saying anything or making a show of it, leadership shifted to Canfield. The Mexicans showed him respect rather than general indifference. The *capitán* came to ask Canfield's opinion before he stopped for nooning or to make camp. The immigrants gave way each time he rode back to the rear of the train. They were fascinated, yet they feared him.

The Mexicans had a name for him now, though they did not use it in his hearing. They called him the Hawk.

I had seen larger towns than Stonehill but none more alive for its size. Its streets were crowded by great tarpaulin-covered freight wagons drawn by as many as sixteen mules or horses; by the creaking Mexican carts with their many spans of muscled oxen. Between the wagons, often seeming in some jeopardy of being crushed by the huge wheels, walked or ran people of all descriptions, a variety I thought would rival New Orleans. They all seemed to have someplace to go or something important to do.

Here, Canfield told me, two busy trails came together, one from Galveston and Indianola on the coast, the other from Mexico and the Rio Grande, joining here for the journey on to San Antonio, and north and west. This town was still new enough that the unpainted lumber had not yet darkened on some of its buildings. The courthouse, a simple two-story affair built like a square wooden box, stood in the center of the activity and told one and all that this was the seat of a newly organized county which destiny had marked for greatness.

It seemed to me that an inordinate percentage of the business houses were dramshops of some kind. The word "saloon" had not come into common usage as it would later on.

Canfield said, "One can become poor dealing in the necessities of life, but only a bad choice of location can make a pauper of a whisky merchant. For that purpose, there is not a bad location in Stonehill."

A newly-painted sign over the door of a general store and post office declared: "Stonehill, the Jewel of Texas—Brightest Point in the Lone Star."

"A pesthole," Canfield countered.

I was too impressed by the busy, bustling aspect of the town to accept that judgment at face value. I said, "It must have a place."

"It does. If it were in my power, that is where I would send it."

I was in no position to argue the point, for he had been here before the town. I said, "I'll wager I can find employment."

"Perhaps. But you came in with a Mexican cart train, and

that will go against you. A lot of local money is tied up in freight wagons and the wagoner trade."

Once he broached this matter I began to pay attention to the people who watched us. I saw hostility in some faces, now that I began looking for it. The experience shook me. I had never had reason to encounter hostility back home. On the delta I had only friends. In Texas barely a week, I already had enemies. I was unprepared for so much progress.

As we passed a dramshop a young man strode out to meet us. Perhaps the word "strode" is too bold, for he weaved a bit. He had a broad and easy smile, and he waved at Thomas Canfield. "Hello, big brother," he shouted.

Thomas' eyes crackled. His voice was sharp. "Kirby! What are you doing in town?"

"I came to help you unload your goods."

"You were needed more at home."

Kirby Canfield had not shaved in days, but his beard was still soft and boyish. So was his manner. Thomas' harsh rebuke seemed not to touch him at all. He kept his grin.

"You're late," he said. "I thought you would be here yesterday."

"I suppose," Thomas said severely, "that you came the day before that, just to be sure?"

"I try to do my part."

"And so you've been drinking and gambling in this town for two days?"

"Not gambling," Kirby Canfield smiled. "You only gamble when you lose." He stuck his hands into his pockets and jingled a collection of coins. "You have your talents, brother, but you've never seen fit to acknowledge mine."

Thomas gave him no ground. "Since you came to work, I'll see that you do."

"Give me a stirrup," Kirby said, "and I'll swing up behind you."

"You'll walk, and burn the whisky out of your blood."

We had kept moving all this time. Thomas rode up beside the Mexican teamster on his lead cart and pointed leftward at the next corner. His two carts pulled out of the train. The other carts lumbered along, filling the gap we had left.

The immigrants at the rear of the train attracted considerable attention from the townspeople. As they came up even with us the patriarch of the group nodded gravely and acknowledged Thomas Canfield, thanking him with a gesture and a few strange words. Thomas nodded back, but his eyes searched through the immigrants until they found the girl. I saw a long, silent look pass between them. Thomas turned his head and watched a minute or two after they had gone past us.

"Good luck," he said, too quietly for her or the others to have heard if they had been able to understand him.

We proceeded down the heavily rutted street to a small frame storage building set apart from the principal business district. It was not properly a store, for Thomas kept no store hours. I found when I got to know him better that such a thing was against his nature. This was simply a spartan little warehouse where he could meet a prospective implement customer at their mutual convenience for an exchange of goods and coin of the realm. He went there only on arrangement and stayed only so long as was necessary. Most Stonehill business was strictly for cash. Credit was hard for the borrower to find and for the lender to enforce, because this was a horseback society, always moving.

I helped unload the carts, but Thomas saw to it that his brother did the heaviest lifting. I had not entirely recovered from the effects of the sea trip and was soon tired. Nor was I an employee of Thomas Canfield; my only obligation was gratitude. During the last part of the unloading process I sat on a rough bench with Thomas while Kirby and the Mexicans finished the work. Kirby sweated so much that he appeared to have been caught in a rainshower. Thomas showed him no sympathy, though Kirby expressed a certain good-natured sympathy for himself.

A carriage approached, drawn by a pair of matched bays. On the seat hunched a thin man of middle age, dressed rather well by the standards of the time and place, though he would have been considered threadbare in the better delta towns. Beside him sat a young woman who quickly took my attention. About my age, she was brown-eyed and brown-haired and had a smile like sunshine. That smile was for Thomas Canfield, however, not for me.

Thomas stood up as the carriage came to a stop. In his eyes was a respect I had not seen him give to anyone else in the few days I had known him. "Good morning, Laura. Good morning, Mr. Hines."

I remembered seeing the Hines name on the general store and post office back on the main street. "Good morning, Thomas," the man answered. He touched the brim of a dusty Eastern hat. He returned Thomas' respect in kind. "I see you have brought in another shipment. If ever I were to give thought to selling farm implements, you would probably undersell me." No malice or resentment was detectable in his voice.

Thomas came dangerously near smiling. "I would if I could, sir."

"That is as it should be. A bit of competition helps hold greed in check and keep us honest."

The girl had never taken her eyes from Thomas. I had just as well not been standing there for all she saw of me. I wished she were more observant. She said, "I hope you will come some day for Sunday dinner, Thomas."

"I hardly know when Sunday comes," he replied. I could tell that he liked her, but I did not see the same look in his eyes that he had given the Polander girl.

She said, "I'll have to send you a calendar."

"That would be nice," he said. By the tone of his voice, though, I knew he would not be waiting in suspense.

Hines said to Thomas, "My best regards to your good mother." He fingered his gray-tinged muttonchop whiskers as he briefly appraised first Kirby and then me, showing us no ill will, at least. He flipped the reins and set the team moving. Laura Hines turned and looked back over her shoulder, but only at Thomas, not at the rest of us.

Thomas stared after them. "Even Sodom and Gomorrah had a few good people. Linden Hines started this town. He's like a father with a wild son he can't control." He glanced at Kirby. "Or a man with a brother."

He paid the cartmen in silver. There was considerable bowing and beaming and wishing of happy times. At least, that seemed the gist of the talk. The only Spanish I had learned was a few words of profanity that had seemed effective upon the oxen.

Once the Mexicans had taken their leave, I decided it was time I did the same. Unless I found a source of income shortly, I would have to learn to live without eating. I told Kirby Canfield it had been a pleasure to make his acquaintance. I shook Thomas Canfield's hand and thanked him for his courtesies.

He frowned. "I've already told you to expect nothing from this town."

I assured him I intended to stay only long enough to replenish my thin purse, then proceed to San Antonio or farther into the interior. He thanked me for my help in fighting the raiders, though I had only fired some wild shots. I hoisted my little roll of blankets across my shoulder on a short rope and picked up the rifle Thomas had said I was entitled to. I started up the street, looking hopefully at each business house, trying to decide which might offer employment befitting the talents of a delta farm boy. This place was a long way from the cotton fields, both in miles and in character.

I tried six or seven places and met the same cold response at every one. Some mentioned that they had seen me in bad com-

pany. Others implied it or showed it with their eyes. I still had
a little money but resolved to preserve it at all costs. I found a
small place which advertised itself as a restaurant and volunteered to chop wood in return for a meal. The proprietor expressed some reservations about my strength for the work but
said as an act of kindness he would feed me. All I had to do in
return was to chop about half a cord of mesquite wood piled in
the back. I accepted with proper gratitude. I was inclined to eat
first and work afterward, but he expressed the opinion that a laborer performed best on an empty stomach.

It might have been cheaper for him had he allowed me to eat
first. By the time I had chopped the wood I had a ruinous appetite. With no shame whatever, I filled my plate to its edges and
sat down to the task. I was well into my second helping when a
rough-looking teamster came in. Almost immediately his attention went to my rifle, leaning in the corner. He whispered to the
proprietor, who had been morosely studying my progress with
his foodstuffs.

The proprietor did not give me a chance to fill my plate a
third time. He picked it up as I finished the last bite, and he
stood waiting for my coffee cup. I complimented him on his
skill in the kitchen, picked up my rifle and bedroll and went
outside.

There I was confronted by the teamster who had been in
the restaurant. With him were Branch Isom and ten or a dozen
more. Had I known more about the character of Stonehill I
would have brought up the rifle to a strong defensive posture
then and there. It would have been all bluff, however. The rifle
was not loaded.

Isom's eyes were narrowed and cold. "You're the boy that
wanted to be paid to come up from Indianola."

I bristled a little. "And you are the gentleman who offered to
let me pay for the privilege of working."

Isom's gaze fell to the rifle. "Where did you get that?"

I realized he knew very well. I said, "Some raiders attacked the cart train I was with. One of them left it there."

I doubted that these men knew for certain that the raider had been killed. Looking from one hostile face to another I decided my life would not be worth a secondhand chew of tobacco if I told them.

Isom said, "I believe you stole it."

"I picked it up on the field of battle." I had read somewhere about the spoils of war belonging to the victors, but this did not seem an appropriate time to go into history.

A teamster said, "It's Fitz's rifle, all right. Got his initials carved on the stock."

Isom took a step toward me and stopped. I could see little of his eyes because of the heavy red brows. "What happened to the man who carried it?"

I suspected they had guessed but were not quite certain. It was not my place to bear ill tidings to strangers. I said, "You should know better than I do. You were with him."

I did not see Isom's fist coming, but a sledgehammer could not have struck me harder. I staggered backward with lights flashing in my eyes. He hit me again and I landed on my back, on top of my rolled-up blankets. The rifle fell. I acted by instinct, though not very well. I got to my feet, took a couple of hard swings at him and missed, then was knocked down again for my trouble. I scrambled at him from hands and knees and managed to get both arms around his legs, tripping him. We rolled in the dirt. I hit him three or four times, but never as hard as he hit me. From the first it was clear I was going to lose.

Toward the end I was seeing through a painful blur. Thomas and Kirby Canfield had walked up. Kirby seemed about to come to my aid, but Thomas held him back. It was my fight.

It came to me later, when I knew him better, that Thomas Canfield was not a crusader. He did not go rushing about looking for other people's fights. He would have taken no part in the Mexicans' fight against the raiders had he not had a shipment of freight on their carts. He took no part in my fight. Had it been over something or someone who belonged to him, he would have.

At last I was lying beaten, hardly able to move. Branch Isom had his knee on my chest. "Now, boy, you tell me what happened to Fitz."

Thomas Canfield said evenly, "Let him up, Isom."

Isom glanced at him with uncertainty. "This is not your affair."

"I believe it is. *I* killed your man Fitz."

Isom pushed to his feet. "He wasn't my man, Canfield. He quit me on the trail."

Canfield's voice was as cold as January. "Only after I shot him. He was your man, Isom. You led him, and you killed a man of mine who was worth more than a dozen of you and the scoundrels who hang around you in this scabby town."

It came to me suddenly that they were about to try to kill one another, and I was lying on the ground between them. But I could not move. I lay there trembling, not able even to breathe.

Isom said, "You're wrong, Canfield."

Canfield's voice dropped lower. "You're a liar."

Fury flashed in Isom's eyes, and his hand went to the pistol. As I watched, he drew it from the holster, then stopped, the muzzle pointed more or less at me. The fury in his eyes melted to something else, to uncertainty, to fear.

I turned my head toward Canfield and saw that his pistol was up and aimed straight at Isom. His finger was tight on the trigger. In his eyes was a cold hatred far removed from the quick fury that had drained from Isom's. I could see his finger turning white. I lay paralyzed with fear of my own, knowing that if he fired, Isom's last convulsive act might be to kill me.

Isom tried to bring up the muzzle of his pistol but could not.

He seemed frozen, staring into the face of death. After what seemed an age, he let his pistol slip back into its holster.

Weakly he said, "I see no reason to kill you, Canfield."

For another heartbeat, Canfield seemed still determined to fire, but the moment had slipped away from him. Isom's hand lifted clear, showing he was no longer a threat.

If Canfield had intended to shoot him, he had waited too long. For a moment he had had all the excuse he needed. No one could have blamed him. Now that moment was gone.

Isom swallowed. His eyes cut away from Canfield, betraying his fear. From where I lay, I could see his legs tremble even if others could not.

Canfield lowered his pistol reluctantly. Regret was in his eyes, regret that he had not followed through when the moment was right. I could not know, then, how he would grieve in later years over that missed opportunity.

Isom backed slowly away, trying to recover the lost bravado, to deny he had shown the feather. He reached for strength but never quite found it. His shaky voice gave him away. "You watch what you say about me, Canfield. I won't stand still for your slander."

Canfield said nothing. There was no need, for he had made his point and had shown himself the stronger man.

Isom watched narrowly until the rancher's pistol finally returned to its holster. Only then did Isom turn away, walking unsteadily into the nearest dramshop. Some of the dozen or so men followed him. Others simply pulled back to some distance and kept watching. Isom's defeat had been their own, for now at least. The sense of humiliation clung to them.

Kirby Canfield was the first to speak. The tension drained away, and he laughed uneasily. "You beat him, big brother, in front of everybody. That should be the last trouble we'll ever have from Branch Isom."

Thomas' rejoinder was severe. "If you believe that, then you're a fool. He'll have to get back at us now or leave here for

good." He turned to me, catching me under the arms and helping me to wobbly feet. "You put up a good fight, Sawyer, for a
boy in your condition. I should have stopped it sooner. In a
way it was my fight, not yours."

The two Canfields helped me away. It would have been easy
for the remaining Isom crowd to have shot any or all of us in
the back, for the Canfields did not deign to look behind them,
and I could not. After a little while they sat me down on the
edge of a wooden porch at the Hines store. "Go fetch the
wagon here," Thomas ordered.

When Kirby went to obey, Thomas said to me, "I told you
you'd find no friends in this town."

Weakly I acknowledged his perception.

He went on, "I can't pay you much because I have little cash
money. But there's room for you at our place if you want to
work and are in no hurry to run up a fortune."

I told him I would consider staying at least awhile. It was
becoming plain to me that I should learn a lot more about this
country before setting myself loose upon it, alone. In truth, I
felt as if I were crawling beneath a sheltering arm.

I rested the first couple of days in and about the old double
cabin and gorged myself upon the simple but good cooking
done by Thomas Canfield's mother. She was a small, spare
woman bent at the shoulders by a life of hard work. She said a
thing or two that indicated Mr. Canfield—Thomas' father—had
been dead several years. She said nothing about how he had
come to die, and I did not ask. I was gradually coming around
to the notion that when Texas people wanted to talk to you
about something, *they* would introduce the subject.

After those first days of shameful indolence I went to work
clearing mesquite and other brush from a flat, deep-soil pasture
Thomas was preparing to break for the plow. He was resolved
to increase his cultivated acreage in the coming spring. It soon
became apparent to me why he had so little money. Every bit

of cash which came his way—above what went for immediate
necessities—was converted almost immediately into land, wherever he could find any for sale within riding distance of the
home place. His properties were scattered like the squares on a
checkerboard, and he was constantly striving to solidify them.

He gave me the first of many lectures I was to hear from him
about the importance of owning land. I suspected he had in-
herited the hunger from his father, who had taken up the original ground in the Canfield name.

"Land is where the real wealth lies. Businesses come and go.
Towns grow and then die. But the land is constant. Whenever
you have the chance, Sawyer, grab onto the land and hold it.
Everything else is just rainbow."

Over the next month or so he sold most of the implements
stored in Stonehill and ordered more out of New Orleans. The
profit went to buy a parcel of unbroken rangeland from absen-
tee survivors of a San Jacinto battle veteran who had received
the property as a reward from the Republic of Texas, before
statehood, but had never lived on or worked it.

All winter he talked of making up another expedition into
the Indian country farther west, so he could bring in another
stock of mustang ponies to break and sell. The wild horses,
subsisting on winter range, would be at their weakest and could
not so easily outrun those helped along with grain. But we
remained so busy that spring planting time caught us, and we
could not go.

Some people like Thomas Canfield seem born to lead, to ac-
cumulate and build. Others, like Kirby, seem content enough to
follow and to work for someone else. Kirby lacked his brother's
passion for acquisition. He tended toward observation of the
lilies in the field, toward savoring the full flavor of each day
which came to him. He seldom deferred today's pleasures in the
hope of accumulating interest for a greater payment at some
vague future time. He worked hard and carried his share of the
load, for to do less was considered a poor show of one's man-

hood in those days. But in the evenings when Thomas busied himself with ledgers and survey records and maps, when Mrs. Canfield spun yarn on an old wheel so they wouldn't have to buy cloth, Kirby was likely to be playing an old fiddle or proving the dexterity of his fingers with a deck of cards. He even taught me how to play.

Back home it had been given to me as holy writ that cards were a device invented by the devil to aid him in stealing men's souls. Kirby never took advantage of me by playing for money. We played only for pleasure. Still, the old preachments plagued me every time my fingers closed upon the cards.

Kirby would laugh. "Anything is made a bit more pleasant for being just a little wicked."

Occasionally he liked to slip away to Stonehill. Although he was a grown man and Thomas had no authority to prevent him, Kirby usually waited until Thomas was away from home for a day or two. He tried to get me to go with him, but I declined the first couple of times. I had vivid recollections of my rough experience in that town. Finally, however, I succumbed to temptation, for the town with its bustle and great activity was always an object of curiosity. Most of the people who had frowned before had forgotten my past associations. They seemed to remember only that I was connected with the Canfields. This threw a thin protective cloak over me.

I found that Thomas Canfield was not the only ambitious person in the Stonehill region. Branch Isom, the freighter, had bought out a dramshop and operated it in addition to his line of wagons. He had built an extension onto the back and set it up with gaming tables. These drew Kirby Canfield as a bin of oats draws a frisky young horse. He tried his luck there and more often than not found it good. I was glad I had never played him for money.

Had he chosen to do so, I think he might have sustained himself by his proficiency with cards. But when I suggested the possibility, he said, "I play for diversion. If I ever depended on it for a living it would be pleasant no longer."

On our way home we rode by the little fenced cemetery on the slope above the ranch headquarters. Kirby dismounted and took off his hat while he stared at a headstone. "Papa was the only one who understood about me," he said, the fun suddenly gone from him. "I think he had a little of that streak in him too. If he hadn't, he might still be alive."

It was the first good chance I had had to ask, "What happened to him?"

"When things got too thick around here for him, he would occasionally ride over to Stonehill for a few drinks. It was a harmless thing, or should have been; he never did it very often. One night he just happened to get caught in the middle when a couple of teamsters started shooting at one another. Papa was the first man killed."

"The teamsters . . . did they die too?"

Kirby nodded. "One of them went down in the fight."

"And the other one?"

Kirby looked away. "Thomas found him."

We were struggling with our work oxen, breaking the hard ground for spring planting, the day the San Antonio priest came to us. His face was grave. He spoke good English, though his accent was heavy and I had to listen with care to understand him. He nodded to Kirby and me, but he seemed to sense on sight that Thomas was the man in charge.

"Are you aware," he asked Thomas, "of the desperate situation in New Silesia?"

I knew that was the name of the village the immigrants had built for themselves. Though it lay only about ten miles north, my work had never taken me there.

Thomas said, "I didn't know there *was* a situation."

"If you care for your fellow man," the priest told him, "you should go and see for yourself. Surely you can do something to help those poor people in their misery."

Thomas' face clouded. "Have you been to other places around here for help?"

"I just came from Stonehill. I find the town well named. The merchant Hines has pledged some help, but most of the others say let those people go back where they came from."

Thomas frowned. "Perhaps they should."

"They cannot. Nothing is left for them in the old country. They have not the means to move ten miles. They must stay."

I had seen slaves living in little more than chicken coops on some delta farms where owners took insufficient care of their property. But at their worst most of them fared better than the people we found as we rode into the immigrant village. The newest arrivals had come in the dead of winter and for shelter had been able to do little more than dig into the cold ground, covering the holes with a matting of thatched grass for a roof to try to see them through to spring. Some who had been there longer had built picket houses, copied after the style of Mexican *jacales,* but these with their mud chinking and brush roofs had been poor shelter against the elements.

Ragged children bunched before the miserable hovels, watching with wide and hungry eyes as we passed. It occurred to me that there were few dogs. Children without dogs were like coffee without sugar, or meat without salt. These families had nothing to feed to a dog. Adults crossed themselves as the priest passed them. Both men and women still wore the same odd clothing I had seen among the immigrants who had accompanied us from Indianola to Stonehill.

It was as if I had been picked up suddenly and transported to some strange land beyond the seas. I found it little wonder that people in Stonehill had nothing complimentary to say about this alien settlement. What we do not understand, we reject.

Thomas Canfield's face became like stone, grim and brooding. He looked carefully at each person he saw on the street. At length he asked the priest, "Where are the ones who came in last?"

"You have seen most of them. A few are out breaking their fields."

"There was one family . . . I don't know their names. They had a girl, sixteen or seventeen."

The priest considered. "The Brozeks, perhaps. They have a girl named Maria."

"Show me."

We rode almost to the end of the village. Thomas saw the girl before the rest of us did, and he straightened. She was sweeping the bare ground clean in front of a crude dugout, using a rough broom fashioned out of dried weeds tied to a mesquite branch. It seemed a futile thing to be sweeping bare ground, but it was at least an effort at cleanliness. It was an act of defiance.

Her eyes went right to Thomas and held there. The two stared at each other a minute, and Thomas took off his hat. "Hello" was all he said. She responded in words I did not know, in a voice almost too soft to hear. It struck me that she was thinner than on the trip from Indianola, and even then she had been barely large enough to cast a decent shadow.

Thomas said to the priest, "Tell her we are going to help. We don't have much except cattle, but we'll bring some of those. They'll have milk and meat."

The priest translated. The girl never took her eyes from Thomas more than a moment. She said something which the priest told us was simply "thank you."

As we rode away, Thomas turned in the saddle and looked back.

We gathered some of his cattle, which he had scattered widely on the land he owned and upon unused land which lay between his tracts. He picked some recently calved cows which had udders swollen with milk. "They are wild, and they'll have to be tied, but they'll give milk for the children," he said. He picked some fleshy long-aged calves and yearlings, though after a hard winter none were really fat. It was a sacrifice of some dimensions, but he did not grieve over it. We drove about twenty beeves and as many cows into the stricken village.

There we found Linden Hines and his daughter Laura distributing flour and coffee, and some woolen bolt goods out of his mercantile store. Thomas tipped his hat to Laura, whose face glowed at the sight of him. Gravely he shook hands with Hines. "It's good to see you, sir. I knew you would be the only man in Stonehill with enough Christian charity to bring anything here."

Hines shook his gray head. "This isn't all mine. Branch Isom wouldn't want it talked about, but he contributed part of it."

Thomas blinked. He seemed somehow angered, somehow affronted. "Isom? What can he ever expect to get out of *this* place?"

The priest walked from the small crude building which passed for a church. He smiled as he came and thanked Thomas for being a man of his word. "You may have saved some poor children from dying, and others from becoming orphans."

Thomas looked for a place to pen the cattle. A couple of the Polander men hurried ahead of us, pointing and talking in their language until they reached a rough enclosure built of mesquite. They let down the crooked bars that served as a gate and helped haze the cattle in.

Most of the village people had gathered, all trying to talk to us at once. Laura Hines had followed along and stood at the edge of the crowd, saying nothing but watching Thomas with admiration. To me the talk was a babble, though the priest did not have to translate the gratitude, the smiles on haggard faces. He went through a ceremony which I surmised was some form of blessing on the gift of cattle.

The girl Maria was there with some younger brothers and

sisters and her parents. I remembered them from the trip. She smiled at Thomas, and he smiled back.

I glanced at Laura Hines. She looked puzzled, her smile gone.

Thomas beckoned the priest. "Father, I want you to talk to this girl for me, please. Tell her that if it is all right with her, and with her father, I'd like to come here and call on her."

The priest showed misgivings. Clearly he thought Thomas was asking a price for the cattle. "These are a moral people," he said.

"If I had not thought so I would not have helped them. There are already more than enough of the other sort in this country."

"But you cannot even talk to her."

"We'll talk. You just ask her."

The priest spoke. The girl turned excitedly to her parents. I could see the question in the eyes of the older couple as they stared at Thomas. Perhaps they remembered the coldness they had seen in him as he waited for the wounded raider to talk or to die. But that had to be weighed against his sacrifice in bringing cattle here to feed the hungry. If this was the judgment they were making, the cattle won.

I suppose girls where she came from were trained to be reserved, and she tried. But her eyes, brown and big and pretty, sparkled with delight.

Thomas said to the priest, "I lose track of time when I am busy. What day is this?"

"Friday."

Thomas nodded. "Tell her I will be here Sunday."

I looked around for Laura Hines, but she was gone.

CHAPTER 3

He was there that Sunday and almost every other for a long time. His one suit was tight on him because it had been made several years earlier, before hard work and maturity had muscled him. But few people there in those days kept up with styles. A tight suit or a threadbare one was better than no suit at all. Many people had none at all.

Thomas did not allow romance to spoil his penchant for hard work or for business. He did not *send* Kirby and me out to work, he *led* us, and usually he did more than either of us. Even with all his other responsibilities he managed to sell some farming implements, to keep the cash turning. Sometimes he willingly allowed profit opportunities to escape him, however. He distributed a number of plows and other tools among the Silesians with the understanding that they would pay when they were able. I was convinced he would never realize a dollar and would have to mark these in his blue-backed ledger as a gift, along with the cattle. I did not know at the time how dedicated these immigrants were both to hard work and to their own good word.

When the planting was done and the new calves branded and worked, we had a while when the home duties could be allowed to slacken. True, the fields would need to be cultivated to keep the emerging crops free of weeds, but Amadeo Fernandez's widow and two sons still lived on the place. The boys were big enough that together they did a man's work. Thomas said we could leave the cropland to them for a while. It was time to ride west and gather mustangs.

The thought set my heart to pounding. It had seemed adventuresome, far out in the future. But suddenly confronted with the fact of going, I realized with a chill that we would be venturing into Indian country. Kirby assured me with card-player confidence that the chances were two to one we would never see an Indian. I found myself looking with trepidation at the third chance.

Thomas told Kirby he was to stay to look after their mother and supervise the place. Kirby's face flushed with a touch of anger, but he said nothing. The Fernandez boys begged to go, but Thomas told them gently that they might do so the next time.

Mrs. Canfield cooked us a good breakfast before daylight of a Sunday morning, and we set out at daylight, each riding a good horse and leading another. We rode by New Silesia, for Maria would be expecting Thomas. She did not expect him so early, however, and he had to wait restlessly for her to come out of mass at the little church. I had not seen her since the day we had delivered the cattle. She had fleshed out a little, with color in her cheeks and a warm smile in her eyes. The smile was not for me, of course.

She had learned some random words of English. Thomas even spoke some words of Polish. At least I assumed that was what they were, because they did not have the sound of Spanish. It occurred to me, though I was inexperienced in that field, that romance can be an educational endeavor.

I tried to find something else to occupy my interest and give the couple privacy, but Thomas called me back before I strayed far. It does not take long to see all one wants of poverty.

In the limited vocabulary they had established between them, Thomas had made Maria understand he was going away for a while. She was tearful, but it was the way of her people that the man made the decisions and the woman quietly agreed; at least that was the way they made it appear. When we left, Thomas kept looking back so long as the village was in sight. The girl stood there by herself, watching as long as there was anything to see.

We rode by a Mexican settlement somewhat farther west and picked up three Mexicans Thomas had known for years. They were good, dependable hands, he said, though given to extortion when it came to wages. They wanted fifty cents a day. He got them to agree to forty, and to furnish two horses apiece for the work.

Only two of them actually rode away with us. The third disappeared into the brush. Thomas seemed to have no concern, so I decided not to worry about it. That night, when we camped, that Mexican came into camp with a fourth man, a tall, bewhiskered countryman with one eye gone and the other fierce as a panther's. He shook hands with Thomas, stared at me with silent suspicion, ate a little supper and disappeared back into the brush.

Thomas let me simmer on my unasked questions awhile before he told me, "That's Bustamante. The law is interested in his whereabouts."

I did not doubt that. "What for?"

"Murder."

"And you'd take him with us?"

"He's one of the best mustang runners you'll ever see. Out yonder, there is no law."

That was a point which worried me.

Whatever preconceived notions I had had about adventure quickly faded in the bright sunlight of reality. Catching mustangs was mostly hard work and very little adventure. Thomas at one point remarked that the Indians did not often bother with the mustangs except to shoot them for meat. It was much easier to take broken horses from the settlements than to catch and break mustangs for themselves. After a few days I could see why.

A set of traps and corrals Thomas had built on previous excursions was still standing but in need of repair to be able to

hold wild horses. The task involved more digging, lifting and
cutting than riding. An Indian battle would have seemed a welcome relief from all that manual labor. Once we finished re-
pairing and extending the corrals, we started hunting mustangs.
My first reaction upon the initial sighting was disappointment.
They were small animals, ungainly in appearance, their manes
long and shaggy, their tails bristling with burrs and almost
dragging the ground. But they were deceptively swift of movement, elusive as jackrabbits. The chase had its moments of
thrill and hard spurring as we brought the wily horses down to
the wings and traps, but those moments were quickly over and
gone. Then the hard work started again.

I did not sleep much the first couple of nights, worrying
about Indians murdering us in our blankets. I did not like Bustamante's looks either. I was glad we had no money with us, for
I was convinced he would have murdered us all for a dollar and
a half. At times, the look in his single eye hinted he might even
do it for nothing more than the pleasure. I quit worrying about
the Indians before I quit worrying about Bustamante. I became
convinced that if any Comanches had come upon us and had
seen what we were doing, they would have left us alone.
Thomas had said Indians did not bother the insane.

Once we had caught a band of horses, Thomas would pick
out those he thought might have market value in the settlements. We let the others go. For seed, he said. We then set in to
rough-break the good ones so we could take them home without undue trouble. This involved, more than anything, teaching
them respect for rope and halter. It was with the *reata,* a
leather rope, that Bustamante showed his greatest skill; I mar-
veled at how he could judge distance so well with one eye. He
would catch a horse by its forefeet and trip it, let it up and trip
it again until it became educated to the power of the rope.
After the horses had been through enough of this bruising exercise, we placed makeshift hackamores on them, tied them
firmly to posts or trees and scared them into running against the

end of the tie rope, jerking them back or jerking them down until the hackamores had rubbed their heads raw. It seemed brutal, but it was a traditional Mexican system for teaching them that the rope was master, always to be obeyed.

We even rode some of them, or attempted to. The Mexicans were good at this, especially the fearless Bustamante, but I invariably hit the ground faster than I had left it. Thomas commented that I could ride little better than I could shoot and suggested that I quit trying. He did not want to take me home with a broken leg and lose my services altogether. I conceded the wisdom of his advice.

Exhaustion made me sleep well at night, but I remained watchful during the day. An Indian could not have gotten closer than a quarter mile without my seeing him. I gradually put aside most of my dread of the dark Bustamante, too, though I contrived whenever possible to keep Thomas between him and me. When we finally haltered our catch and tied each animal to a long lead rope for the trip home, I felt an odd mixture of both relief and regret that we had not seen a single Comanche. I thought how disappointing it would someday be to my grandchildren—if I ever had any. I decided I would do like most other garrulous old liars and make up a story to please them.

The Mexicans left us for their own homes. Bustamante disappeared into the brush as quietly as he had first come.

I expected Thomas to go first by New Silesia to see Maria, but he fooled me. He rode by the fields to see if they had been properly cultivated during our lengthy absence. He expressed pleasure in the hoe work done by the Fernandez boys, Juan and Marco. That pleasure faded when he found out Kirby was in Stonehill and had been for three days.

The little Mrs. Canfield rocked restlessly and knitted on some kind of black shawl on the breezy dog run of the double cabin. She said, "I tried to tell him he'd better stay away from town. Been a right smart of trouble."

Thomas stiffened. "What kind of trouble?"

"Fights between the wagon people and the cart people. Been some men killed on the trail and one or two in town. Government's got soldiers patrolling the trails now, guarding carts and wagons. A patrol was by here just yesterday, trailing some raiders who got away. They had burned up a good part of a cart train headed for San Antonio."

Thomas said, "That doesn't concern us."

"Might concern *you*," the old woman said, laying the knitting in her lap. "Didn't you send orders to Indianola for implements to be sent to Stonehill on Francisco Arroyo's carts?"

Thomas blinked in sudden concern. "I did."

"We heard Francisco got hit two days short of Stonehill. Lost three men and four carts. That's how come Kirby went to town, to find out how much of a loss you taken."

Thomas Canfield seldom wasted anything, including profanity. He employed a few choice words suited to the occasion and started toward town. He shouted back at me to take care of our mustangs.

Next morning I was in a corral with the horses we had captured when I saw two men coming in something of a hurry. I thought at first they were Thomas and Kirby, but they were strangers, or almost so. I had seen both in the Isom dramshop when I had been there with Kirby. They were rough fellows, the kind you do not normally associate with hard labor and honest endeavor. They stopped to water their horses, and they eyed our mustangs as if contemplating a trade. It occurred to me that they could make any trade they might decide upon, for my rifle was at the house. But they seemed to agree after some consultation that the horses they rode were more dependable than the wild ones in our corral. They proceeded in a north-easterly direction at a strong trot that could carry a man many a league between sunup and sundown.

Perhaps an hour later a number of horsemen approached from the same direction where I had first espied the two. This time, for precaution, I hurried down to the cabin and fetched my rifle.

They were blue-uniformed government troops, with Thomas and Kirby riding at the lead. They came directly to the place where I stood, halfway between the log house and the pens. Thomas did the talking, what little was done.

"We are following two men."

I pointed out where they had gone.

An officer said, "We can take the trail from here, Mr. Canfield. You have been of more than enough service to us."

"I'll stay with you until the job is done," Thomas said sternly. His sharp eyes were on Kirby. "You'll stay here."

Kirby did not argue. His beard was four or five days long, and his eyes showed he had traveled in considerable discomfort. Kirby was ordinarily a jovial sort, but he watched darkly as Thomas led the soldiers northeastward.

He complained, "Thomas doesn't give me credit for anything."

I had no inclination to insert myself into an argument between the brothers, so I did not ask him what his trouble was. He told me anyway. "Thomas lost a good part of his shipment. I hung around town, drinking a lot less than I made out. I figured sooner or later I would hear something, and I did. If it hadn't been for me they wouldn't have known who to go after."

"Then those two raided the cart train?"

"They were in the bunch. A couple more put up a fight in town. The troopers blew their lights out for good."

Long shadows fell behind the soldiers and their mounts as they returned shortly before sundown. They led two very tired horses. Across the saddles, two men were tied belly down on the last horseback trip they would ever make.

Thomas watched somberly as the soldiers watered their weary animals. He said to the officer, "You and your men are more than welcome to camp anywhere that suits you. We'll slaughter a fresh beef for you. You've done a hard day's work."

The lieutenant's shoulders were sagging. "I'd appreciate it, Mr. Canfield. There will be bad feelings in town. I had rather we face it in the daylight, when we can see everybody."

The two bodies were laid out in a shed. Thomas looked at them with no more compassion than if they had been wolves caught chasing calves. A fierceness was in his eyes.

In the morning he lent the soldiers a wagon, for the bodies had stiffened. The officer suggested that it might be just as well to bury them then and there. Thomas said coldly, "Let Stonehill bury its own. This place is for ours."

He had lost about half of his shipment. Losing those implements meant losing land he might have bought with the profits. By the time he forgave these men, if he ever did, the headboards on their graves would probably have rotted away.

Kirby suggested, "I'll follow the soldiers into Stonehill and see what happens."

Thomas' eyes were grim. "No. We'll all stay out of Stonehill. A town which caters to people like that can do without our patronage."

Kirby argued, "We have to have supplies of one kind and another. Stonehill's the only place to buy them."

Thomas nodded. "It doesn't have to be that way. New Silesia is no farther than Stonehill."

"It doesn't even have a store."

"It can have one. There are enough farmers and cattle people in the vicinity to make a store work if someone will finance it. I can get credit in San Antonio. I'll finance it."

That took me by surprise. I remembered his many lectures about the permanence of the land, about the vagaries of towns and retail business. But I realized the store in New Silesia would not be undertaken as a business venture; it was an instrument of revenge.

He rode to New Silesia that afternoon, telling me he might not be back for a few days; he was going from there to San Antonio. He left orders for Kirby and me to keep working with the mustangs, gentling them for sale. It was a week before we saw him again.

The old storekeeper, Linden Hines, was there before Thomas returned. His daughter Laura was driving. I helped her down from the carriage, warming to the quick smile she gave me and the momentary chance to hold her hand. Her father said nothing beyond the fact that he wanted to talk to Thomas, but we could see in his pale eyes that he was troubled. He sat on the dog run, gossiping idly with Thomas' mother, who seemed joyed by the company. They talked of the hardships and the spiritual rewards of earlier times, but his gaze was always to the north, watching for Thomas. I tried to engage Laura in conversation, but her mind was not on me. She was helping her father watch.

When Thomas finally appeared, it was hard to tell whether the old man was cheered or depressed. In an odd way, he seemed both. There was no question, however, about Laura's reaction.

Thomas howdied and shook with Laura and her father. They talked in general circles before the gray-haired storekeeper came down to cases. "I heard you're going to open a store in New Silesia."

Thomas blinked in surprise. "News travels fast."

"I have friends in San Antonio." Hines frowned, looking off across the prairie. "It will hurt my store, of course. I had always regarded us as friends, Thomas."

Thomas studied him in regret. "This is not done with any malice toward you, Mr. Hines. We are friends. But we Canfields have no other friends in Stonehill. I would not grieve if I knew I would never have to set foot in that town again."

The old man nodded. "Then this is done against Stonehill, and not against me?"

"I have never had any wish to hurt you. Or Laura." He

glanced at the girl. There was nothing in his eyes to match what I saw in hers.

The old man asked, "What do you know of the store business, beyond selling farm implements?"

"Nothing." An idea seemed to strike Thomas, and he appeared in some danger of smiling. "I could use a partner who *does* know the business."

"Me?" The old man seemed intrigued by the notion for a moment. But he shook his head. "It would be disloyal to Stonehill. That town is like my own child."

"My parents had two children," Thomas pointed out.

"I could not divide my loyalties. I gave the first breath of life to that town. It has grown away from me, like an unruly son sowing wild oats, but it will outlast that. The wildness will pass."

"I doubt that, sir. There is a malady in it that has rooted too deep. It will never be yours again."

The storekeeper mused, looking at Thomas' mother. "Do you believe you or Kirby could ever do anything so bad that your mother could never forgive you, could never take you back and love you?" He shook his head. "Stonehill is my town."

"It will break your heart, Mr. Hines. Or kill you."

"Not Stonehill. It is my child." He dismissed further argument with a small wave of his hand. "You'll not want to spend your own time running your store, Thomas. I have a young man named Smithers; you've surely met him. There is not always enough for him to do in my place, and I have dreaded having to let him go."

"I would be pleased to have him."

So it was that Thomas Canfield branched out into yet another enterprise. For the next few weeks he spent the larger part of his time in New Silesia, supervising carpenters who put up a frame store building for him. Not all of his time was spent on business, evidently, for when the carpenters had finished the job in town he brought them to the ranch. He set them to building a new house. Thomas was not in the habit of volunteering much information, but in this case it was not necessary. We all knew who the house was for.

Kirby and I kept busy cultivating the crops or peddling mustangs to prospective buyers sent or brought by Thomas. When we had sold what he wanted to sell, Thomas surprised Kirby and me by giving us a bonus. I was not sure what to do with mine.

"Land, Mr. Sawyer," Thomas advised. "Whatever you save, put it into land."

I did. I bought a small piece of unimproved rangeland to the west of New Silesia, paying part in cash—all the cash I had—and signing a note for the rest. Because I had no cattle to turn loose on it, Thomas leased it from me and paid me enough that I was able to make payments to the San Antonio bank which carried the paper.

The night after becoming a landowner, I sewed a new patch atop an old patch on my britches and pondered the glories of wealth in land.

Mrs. Canfield had never met Maria. One Sunday morning Thomas took a wagon to New Silesia and brought Maria back to show her how well the carpenters were doing. He made official what we had known for a long time, that he and Maria would marry when the house was finished. I had worried over what Mrs. Canfield would think of Maria in view of the fact that they could not talk much to each other. The two women fell into each other's arms, and my worry evaporated like spilled water in the summer sun. I was amazed by how much English Maria had learned since the last time I had seen her.

Though we had much work to do, Kirby became restless. We played cards some nights, for matches rather than for money, and he usually won though his heart was not in the game. In his hands a card seemed to turn magically into whatever he wanted it to be. I was little challenge. He tried to teach the Fernandez boys, but they were too young and no challenge at all. He would even have played against Mrs. Canfield, if she would have stood for it, but like my own parents she remained convinced that playing cards were the antithesis of holy Scripture. Whenever she found a deck of cards they went into the blazing cookstove. Fire, she declared, was the proper element for Satan and his instruments.

The wedding was performed in the little church in New Silesia. Most of the Polander people were there. Not all of them could get into the church, but those who couldn't stood outside and listened through the open windows. I was inside but had just as well have been outside for all I understood of the service. The only part I was sure of was when the priest said Thomas and Maria were man and wife.

The only people who came over from Stonehill were Linden Hines and his daughter Laura. She tried hard to keep smiling, but this was more like a funeral to her than an occasion of joy. Kirby stood beside her and held her arm, which I wanted to do but lacked the nerve. That didn't help her.

A broad grin was spread across Thomas' face as he walked out of the church with his new bride on his arm. I had never seen that look on him before, and I never saw it again.

Times had improved some for the Polanders. A wedding was a festive occasion, celebrated by everybody in town, with more food than an army could eat, and more than a little of spiritous liquors, these mostly furnished by Thomas, who ordinarily would not have approved much more than his mother would. A big dance was set for the wedding night. I looked forward to it because I thought finally I would have a suitable opportunity to put my arms around Laura Hines. But when the music started and I looked around for her, she was gone.

Thomas never did anything haphazardly. He even timed the wedding so he would not miss anything important at home while he took Maria for her first trip to San Antonio. The crops were fairly well laid by, and it was too early to brand the new calves; screwworms would have eaten them alive. It should have been the best possible time to have taken a long trip. It would have been, except for Kirby.

I figured out very soon that he had been waiting for Thomas to get so far out of reach that Kirby could do whatever he wanted. He stayed just long enough to wave the newlywed couple on their way, then saddled his horse.

"You take Mother home, Reed," he told me. "I'm going to go find some card players who can keep me from going to sleep in the middle of a game."

I tried to argue him out of it. I told him Thomas wouldn't like it, a point I probably should have kept to myself. It seemed only to urge him on. He didn't say he was going to Stonehill, but that was obvious. He rode off in Stonehill's direction, new suit and fresh shave and all, while I walked along after him, futilely throwing out every argument I could think of. He spurred into an easy lope and left me talking to myself.

His mother wanted to know where he was going. I evaded any direct answer, but she knew anyway; I could tell by the set of her jaw. As we rode along in the wagon together I saw tears come into her eyes. She said, "I used to look forward to the day when my sons were grown, so I would never have to worry about them anymore."

That night I sat down by lamplight and wrote a letter to my own mother in Louisiana, the first one in many months.

I thought Kirby might come back that night, but he was not there for breakfast. Mrs. Canfield said nothing, not about Kirby or anything else. She was normally a fair to middling talker, and I expected her to relive the whole wedding over the breakfast table, but the only time she spoke was to ask me if I wanted more coffee. I didn't; I wanted to get out of that cabin as quickly as I could.

I rode among the cattle all day, looking for screwworm cases. Marco, the older of the Fernandez boys, was with me so we could rope and throw cattle as a team and doctor them where we found them. Juan, the younger, remained in the fields, hoeing out the careless weeds. When I rode up to the shed late in the afternoon, I saw that Kirby's saddle was still not on its rack.

Mrs. Canfield met me at the door, her face uneasy. "Reed, I hate to ask you to ride into Stonehill alone, but I wish you'd go see if you can fetch Kirby home. The devil has many allies in that place."

I ate a hurried supper, then saddled a fresh horse, a young bay named Stepper that Thomas had kept out of that set of mustangs. Almost as an afterthought I shoved a big pistol into my boottop. It was a useless gesture; I probably would never have pulled it. But it gave me a feeling of some security, rubbing a blister on my leg.

Just before dark I began to make out a movement on the town road ahead of me. It was a carriage of some kind, flanked by a couple of riders. For no good reason I could think of, my uneasiness increased. I put the bay mustang into a long trot, which it resisted, almost pitching me.

Linden Hines and his daughter Laura were in the carriage, a couple of Mexicans riding horseback beside them. A wagon followed fifty yards or so behind.

One look at the Hineses' solemn faces told me my uneasiness had been fully justified. Laura began to weep. Her father said evenly, "We are bringing Kirby Canfield home."

I looked back at the wagon, the heart dropping out of me.

The old man's voice went lower. "He was shot down in a gaming place in Stonehill."

I took a grip on the big horn of the Mexican saddle I rode. When the shock had passed a little I asked him who did it.

"A tough named Johnroe. I am told there was some disagreement over cards."

I knew before I asked him. "The gaming place . . . was it Branch Isom's?"

He nodded, seeming a little surprised at my guess. "But Isom had nothing to do with it," he said. "In fact, he was in my store when we heard the shots. Laura can tell you. She was there."

The girl nodded, but she did not look at me.

Convenient, I thought. How could Isom better take out his revenge on Thomas Canfield—a man he was afraid of—than to have someone kill his brother, with Branch Isom himself in the clear?

I had gone out into Indian country and helped hunt mustangs, but I knew this thing was beyond my courage. "You-all going to tell Kirby's mother?"

Hines nodded sorrowfully. "All the way from town I have been trying to decide what to say. The Canfields have been among the best friends I ever had. But my town has cost them dearly."

Laura Hines looked up. "I'll tell her."

I think Mrs. Canfield sensed it before we quite got there. She stood in the dog run, watching the carriage and the wagon. The fact that I was with them told her Kirby was too. Without a word, she just looked at us, and died a little. She never shed a tear, at least where I could see it. Whatever crying she did, she held until Laura had gone into the cabin with her.

Laura came back outside, looking for me. She had been crying, whether Mrs. Canfield had nor not. "Reed, you'll have to go to San Antonio. Thomas has to know."

The trail to San Antonio was an old one, cut by wagons and carts past any counting. I had no trouble staying with it through the long, dark night. My horse gave out toward daylight. I stopped at a stagecoach stand and talked the people into lending me a fresh one. They weren't going to do it until I mentioned Thomas Canfield. They seemed more than willing then, and genuinely distressed when I explained my mission.

Thomas and Maria had a room in the new Menger Hotel, Mrs. Canfield had told Laura. Though I had never been in San Antonio, it was no trouble to find the place. As was the custom in old Mexican towns, all roads led to the center like a wagon spoke leads to the hub. The Menger stood with a squared-off German elegance next to the ruins of the Alamo. Commerce moved up and down that street as if nothing had ever happened there. Hardly anybody seemed to look at that shell-marked old mission except me, and for a minute or two I could look at nothing else, remembering the stories I had heard of the good men who had died fighting there. It seemed somehow sacrilegious that the U. S. Army was using the blood-bought building for a quartermaster depot. But I turned away from the Alamo, for that trouble had been more than twenty years in the past, and my problem was *now*. I made my way around several spans of Mexican burros that struggled to pull a wagonload of heavy freight, and I tied the borrowed horse at the rail in front of the hotel. I dusted myself the best I could with my hat, for the Menger was a place that bespoke gentility. I entered the little lobby, pausing to look up in awe at the balconies that towered high above the ground floor. Even New Orleans could have nothing better or taller than this.

The man at the desk betrayed a touch of German accent when he asked what service he could render me. I told him I had to see Thomas Canfield.

"Mr. Canfield and his lady, they went upon the city out."

"I have to see him," I said. "I have a death message for him."

That got the clerk's full attention, but it did not help me find Thomas. "I wish to help, sir," he apologized, "but I know not where to tell you to seek. Best perhaps you sit here and wait."

The smell of food from the kitchen reminded me I had not eaten. It was coming on noon, but I went into the dining room and asked for breakfast. I sat so I could watch the front door. I put away some ham and three or four eggs, then went back into the lobby and took a soft chair where I could see who came and went. My intentions were good, but the flesh was weak after a night's ride. I drifted off to sleep within minutes after I sat down.

A strong hand shook my shoulder and startled me awake. "Reed Sawyer! What is wrong at home?"

It took me a moment to realize where I was. I stared up into the worried eyes of Thomas Canfield, and beyond him, Maria. There was no easy way to tell him. "Kirby was shot in Stonehill. He's dead."

Maria choked off a cry. Thomas made no sound. I don't think he even blinked. His eyes went fierce, like the night he watched the raider die. "Was it Branch Isom?" he demanded.

"No," I told him quickly, trying to head off that line of thought because I feared he would ride straight to Stonehill and kill Isom, or try. "Mr. Hines said Isom wasn't there. It was somebody named Johnroe."

Thomas seemed to stare right through me. "I know Johnroe. His hand moves as Isom directs it. I suppose the law has done nothing."

"I don't know. I came straight to you." But I knew within reason, just as Thomas did. The law had done nothing and would not.

Thomas gritted, "Something *will* be done." He turned to Maria, softening a little. He gently rubbed away a tear that ran down her cheek. "I am sorry, little girl. We have to go."

She put her head against his chest. "I am sorry also."

Thomas looked back at me. "Is anyone with my mother?"

"Laura Hines. She and her father brought Kirby home."

He nodded. "Laura. Whenever help is needed, she's always there."

It was almost on my tongue to ask him if he did not know why. I caught myself.

It was a fast but silent trip, and I slept a good part of it. Thomas wore out several teams, changing them along the way with people he knew, like those at the stage stop. I don't believe he spoke twenty words beyond what was necessary. Maria sat beside him, but as he had always been and always would be in times of stress, Thomas seemed somehow completely alone,

drawn up within himself like some brooding, secret spirit out of
another time and another life. That Maria accepted this without
protest was a source of wonder to me, but I supposed all things
here seemed mysterious to her compared to that far-off country
she had come from.

Thomas' determined pace brought us to the Canfield place in
the early hours of the night, the last set of horses dripping
sweat. He pulled up in front of the double cabin. Linden Hines
arose from a rocking chair on the dog run and walked out to
meet us. He gave Maria a hand down from the carriage.

Thomas demanded, "How is my mother?"

"Laura finally got her to bed. It has been a long day."

Thomas put a hand on the old storekeeper's shoulder. "For
all of us." We quietly went inside, where Laura arose from her
chair beside Mrs. Canfield's bed. She tiptoed to us, putting a
finger on her lips, but it did no good. Mrs. Canfield called, "Is
that you, Thomas?"

"I'm here," he told her.

The rest of us went back outside, leaving them alone. Maria
stood uncertainly in the doorway, trying to decide if she
belonged in there with her husband, finally coming out with us.
She and Laura stood on the dog run, looking at one another. It
was an awkward moment for me, knowing how both women
felt about that man beyond the door, knowing both had cause
to hate each other. But Maria reached out and touched Laura's
hand.

"You do good thing, Laura. You are good friend."

Laura's voice broke. "I have always been a friend to the
Canfields, all the Canfields. You're a Canfield now."

"Always, you be *my* friend."

If I had any doubts, the funeral at the ranch showed me how
many friends the Canfields really had. Ranchers and farmers
from a wide area came out, along with a goodly part of the
Polander community, many of them afoot. I saw few people
from Stonehill, other than Linden and Laura Hines, and quite a

few of the Mexican oxcart freighters the Canfields had done business with. It struck me as never before how many of the Mexican people were friends of Thomas Canfield. The mustang hunters were there, except Bustamante, and many others I could not remember seeing before. It came to me that the Canfield family had settled here when most of the other people *were* Mexicans. Somehow they had avoided the enmity that beset so many later settlers.

One official representative of Stonehill *was* on hand. The county sheriff and one of his deputies stood at the edge of the crowd, saying nothing but watching everybody, most of all watching Thomas. Thomas was aware of them, but he made no move in their direction or they in his until the services were over, the coffin had been lowered and earth was being shoveled into the grave. Maria was saying something about it was wrong to bury people here; this was not consecrated ground. But Thomas seemed not to hear her. He stood with his mother and Maria, solemnly accepting the condolences of the visitors as they filed by. When all were finished and most had started home, I noticed that many of the Mexicans were staying, huddling to one side. It came to me that every one of them was armed.

Instinctively I knew they were waiting for a signal from Thomas. To them this was another incident in the cart war. True, it had happened to a *gringo,* but the *gringo* had been their friend. Indirectly, in their view, he had died for them.

The sheriff sensed it too. His face was taut; he dreaded having to talk with Thomas. But he could delay it no longer. With hat in hand he spoke his condolences to Mrs. Canfield, then to Thomas. He jerked his head sideways. "Thomas, I wish you'd step out here a ways. We got some talking to do."

Thomas looked at his wife. "Maria, would you please take Mother back to the house?"

Both women looked apprehensively at Thomas, but he assured them there was no trouble. They started reluctantly,

Laura Hines moving in supportively to take Mrs. Canfield's right arm. Thomas watched them go, then turned to the sheriff and the deputy.

"My brother was killed the day before yesterday, Sheriff. What has been done?"

"I've investigated the incident thoroughly. I've talked to all the witnesses."

"Do you have Johnroe in jail?"

"No, the gentleman left the county immediately after the shooting."

"Then you should be after him."

"There is no case against him. All the witnesses told me your brother accused him of cheating at cards, then drew a pistol. They told me Johnroe fired in self-defense."

"Did my brother fire at him?"

The sheriff hesitated. "There was only one shot. Your brother had been drinking. He was slow."

"Not that slow. Your witnesses lie, Sheriff. You know that."

"I do *not* know that."

"You know the whole thing was deliberately planned. You know Branch Isom was behind it."

"Mr. Isom was not even present. Your friend Linden Hines will tell you that, if he hasn't already."

"He told me. Isom used him. He knows it, and I know it, and you know it."

"Mr. Isom is as upset over this as any of us. He wants no trouble, and I want no trouble."

"If you don't do something about Johnroe, I will."

"You'll not find him in Stonehill. I don't want you coming there looking for him, and perhaps getting someone else killed in the process. I don't want trouble with you"—he looked past Thomas at the cluster of waiting Mexicans—"and I don't want trouble with your friends."

"Do I have your word that Johnroe is not in Stonehill?"

"You have. And if he ever shows up there again I'll arrest him. For his own safekeeping."

Thomas had that look in his eyes. "Then you had better find him before I do."

The sheriff blustered, but he could not hold his ground against that hard stare. When he looked down, Thomas turned his back on him. The sheriff appeared to have something more to say but saw the futility of it. He nodded at his deputy, and they mounted their horses. Thomas did not look in the men's direction, but he was listening to the fading sound of the hoofs. After a bit he walked slowly toward the Mexicans. He addressed them in Spanish. I had learned enough to follow a little of it. He thanked them for their sympathy. Past that, the conversation turned from difficult to impossible for me. I heard the name "Johnroe" two or three times, and "Bustamante" once. At first I thought Thomas might be planning to lead them into Stonehill and take the town apart; he was capable of it. But presently the Mexicans dispersed, riding off in the several directions from which they had come.

Life on the ranch settled down to something of routine again, somewhat quieter and grimmer. Thomas was living in his new house with Maria, so I saw less of him than before. When I did see him, he had little to say beyond whatever was necessary to the work at hand. His face had seldom been host to a smile even before Kirby's death. He probably smiled when he and Maria were alone in that house, but I never saw it. His eyes had a steely look that indicated his mind was elsewhere. We took care of the fields and worked the cattle and did what we could to doctor the screwworm cases, but all the time in his mind he was killing Johnroe.

As winter came on, Maria showed signs of gaining weight. She had been so thin that I thought the weight became her. It took a while for me to realize there was more to it than just having food enough. Thomas was busier than ever, partly because of the store in New Silesia. At first he took Maria with him when he had to make a trip to San Antonio, but as she became heavier and nearer her term, she stayed at home. After supper, when he was away, she would come down to the old cabin and sit in a rocking chair beside Mrs. Canfield on the dog run, the two women waiting together for Thomas to come home. Nights when he didn't, Mrs. Canfield would go up to the new house and sleep where she could be near Maria. A couple of times she sent for Mrs. Fernandez with considerable agitation, but nothing happened.

After the second time, Thomas decided to defer all other business trips until the baby was safely "on the ground." He would ride out during the day, but always he was home before dark. Nobody told me anything, but I sensed that the time of delivery was at hand.

The mesquites were putting on their first new leaves, pale green and so thin they seemed transparent. The nights were still cool, but the days were warming enough that it would not be long until time to put corn and cotton into the ground. Maria was so heavy I wondered if she might not be going beyond her normal term.

One morning before daylight I went out to rustle horses and saw a blanket-wrapped form on the ground, near a mesquite-pole corral. As I approached the blanket was suddenly flung aside, and I was looking into the muzzle of a huge pistol. My heart leaped as I recognized the evil eye staring at me over the barrel.

Bustamante.

He recognized me and lowered the pistol. "El patrón," he said. He had come to see Thomas.

I indicated that Thomas was up at the new house, but Bustamante insisted that I bring him down to the corrals.

Thomas came irritably to the door when I knocked, asking me if I didn't know Maria needed her sleep. But his attitude changed to excitement when I told him Bustamante was waiting. He disappeared for only a moment, coming back fully dressed, pulling the long ears of his left boot. He strode briskly ahead of me. I did not see Bustamante until the tall Mexican stepped out from the shadow of a fence. The sight of him was like ice pressed against my chest.

Thomas motioned for me to stop, not to come any closer. I watched them from twenty or thirty paces, catching the tone of an intense conversation but none of the words. At last Bustamante reached inside his shirt and brought forth a leather pouch, hanging around his neck on a string. Thomas loosened the puckerstring and looked into the pouch. He nodded in satisfaction and dropped the pouch on the ground. He brought a handful of coins from his pocket and placed them in Bustamante's outstretched hand.

The men silently shook. Bustamante mounted a long-legged black horse that bore Thomas' brand and loped away, disappearing quickly into the brush.

Thomas leaned down and recovered the pouch from the ground. When he turned I saw a smile, a cold one and mean. He seemed to have forgotten about me, for he was startled to see me standing there.

"Go on about your business, Reed," he said.

I caught up my horse and set out to bring in the mounts for the day's work. As I rode away I saw Thomas at some distance beyond the barn, a shovel in his hand. While I watched, he dug a hole and dropped the pouch into it.

A week later, word drifted down to us from San Antonio that the gambler Johnroe had been killed there. Four days after his arrival, a tall, ugly, one-eyed Mexican had suddenly confronted him on a sidewalk and plunged a knife into him to the hilt. While the man lay dying, the Mexican coldly cut off both of his ears, mounted a black horse and rode away.

Very mysterious, people said. It was probably over a gambling loss.

The news seemed to affect Thomas not at all. Maria had just presented him a son.

He named the boy Kirby.

CHAPTER 4

Because we lived and worked a long way from the larger towns, we let the war slip up on us. We knew, of course, that sectional bitterness had built for years, but mostly we looked on it as a quarrel between the Southern people who owned slaves and the Northern people who wished they did but couldn't. Not many folks down in our part of South Texas had slaves, either; they were too poor for that kind of luxury. So long as the Yankees stayed out of our country and left us alone, we didn't do much except clench our fists a little when we read an occasional angry newspaper editorial. We went right back to our own personal concerns as to whether it would rain, and whether the corn was going to make, and what kind of calf crop would hit the ground. All else was talk, and talk was a surplus commodity without a market.

But war did come, and a lot of us let ourselves get swept up in the emotion of it. We did foolish things, like volunteer for the Texas companies that were joining the Confederate army.

Thomas seemed immune to that kind of emotion. His was reserved for whoever and whatever belonged to him. A war way off in Virginia was too far from his land to be of deep concern to him. He grieved over the thought of all the suffering, all the wreckage that came out of the first fighting, but he did not anger. He told me it was a long way from Texas, and he saw no reason it should ever affect us.

Even Thomas Canfield could be wrong.

Peace, of a sort, had settled over us. The cart war had

ground itself to a standstill. The Texas Rangers and the federal troops—before the bigger war pulled them away—stomped hard on some participants. A few of the worst men on both sides found themselves invited to a quick, quiet hanging, which got everybody else's attention. Most people involved in the feud decided they did not hate each other enough to risk that kind of rough justice.

I half expected the Rangers to fall on Thomas for what had happened to Johnroe. Talk spread around Stonehill that he was somehow responsible. But the lawmen seemed to figure that the killing of Johnroe by some unknown Mexican probably saved them the trouble of a hanging, sooner or later. Or, perhaps they were simply afraid of Thomas. A lot of people were, by then.

I thought Branch Isom might find some way to continue the trouble at no danger to himself, but he did not. Though I took pains to stay out of Stonehill, I heard enough talk to keep up with what went on there. Some of the Mexicans said Isom had fetched himself a bride from San Antonio. He was building a house in Stonehill larger than the one Thomas had built on the ranch for Maria. I figured this was a show of rivalry, but I never mentioned it to Thomas. Nothing brought anger to his eyes like hearing the name of Branch Isom.

The anger came often enough of its own bidding; I did not like to be the one who drew it forth. I much preferred Thomas' company when he sat on the edge of his porch, watching his son take his first faltering steps in the yard, falling over an affectionate pup one of the Fernandez boys had brought to him. Thomas rarely laughed, even with the baby, but the deepening lines in his face would seem to ease, and he would look—for a little while—as young as he really was. He would sit in silence with Maria's loving arm around him and watch that little boy with a feeling akin to worship.

Thomas had stayed out of the cart war except when his own property was involved, and he was determined to remain out of the Confederacy's war too. He said little about it, but he leaned toward the views of old Sam Houston, who tried desperately to keep Texas from seceding and, when it did anyway, retired to his home down in Huntsville to live out his days without ever endorsing the Confederacy.

I tried to see it Thomas' way, but too many things kept pulling at me. I received a letter from home telling me a couple of my brothers had marched out to fight for Jeff Davis. I saw quite a few younger men from around Stonehill and New Silesia do the same thing, laughing and hollering and promising to be home in six months. They could not all be wrong, no matter what Thomas said.

The Polanders avoided being caught up in the war much. They had been in the country too short a time to understand what the fighting was about—if any of us did—and most of them did not know much English. The army recruiters quickly decided they were too dumb to be of much use. The Confederates were so confident about whipping the Yankees in a hurry that they did not want to share the glory with a bunch of foreigners anyway. They saved that honor for the true Southern boys.

My conscience nagged me as more and more men went to war while I stayed home on the ranch. Finally I received a letter telling me one of my brothers had taken down with the fever and died on the way to the fighting. Though he had not reached the battle, my mother considered him a patriot, a martyr to his country. She said nothing about me picking up my brother's sword. I got that idea all by myself. When a cowboy named Bill Eskew announced that he was going to San Antonio to join the war, I decided to go with him.

Thomas took the news with a deep frown. "It's not our fight."

"It's mine," I told him. "I've lost a brother."

"You never could shoot straight. What use will you be?"

But he dropped the argument when he saw I had made up my mind. He shook my hand and told me I would always have a place with him when I came back. Maria—by now beginning to push out in front again—kissed me on the cheek. The old lady Canfield hugged my neck and wet the side of my face with her tears. I tried not to look back as I rode away, but I couldn't help it. Until we passed over the hill, Bill and me, I spent most of my time twisted around in the saddle, trying to fix it all in my mind as if I might not ever see it again.

I almost didn't.

We halfway expected to be wined and dined and have a lot of fuss made over us in San Antonio, but the "new" had worn off by that time. They had already seen a lot of men march away, some west to invade New Mexico and Arizona, the rest east to join up with the main Confederate forces off in Virginia and such. Nobody paid much attention to us or bought us any drinks, and the officers didn't treat us as respectfully as the recruiters had led us to believe. They handled us a lot like we used to treat fresh-caught broncs in teaching them to respect the rope and follow directions. I was considerably disappointed with the war before I ever saw any of it.

I was even more disappointed when I *did* see it. I had seen blood spilled in Texas, but this was not the same. We didn't hear the bands play much. Bill Eskew got shot in the stomach the second battle we got into, and I had to watch him take two days in dying.

There is no point in going on with a lot of detail about my years in the army. Like Thomas had kept saying, it was a long way from Texas and had nothing to do with the Canfields. I got nicked a couple of times, but never anything serious until the last year of the war. A rifle ball struck me in the hip and knocked me off of my horse. When I came back to consciousness I found Yankee soldiers running around me afoot, going the way I had come from. They were too busy to stop either to finish me off or to patch my wound. First time I got the chance I dragged myself into some bushes on my belly and hid. I soaked up most of my coat trying to get the blood stopped. I lay there until almost dark before the Yankees passed me again

going the other way, and some good Reb boys came along in
pursuit.

My hip was a long time healing. They furloughed me home
to Louisiana. That way I was a burden to my family instead of
to the Confederacy, which already had more burden than it
could carry. The war was over before the healing was. Hob-
bling around on crutches, not able to do any respectable work
except patch harness and such, I watched the straggling rem-
nants of a beaten army come limping home a few men at a
time. I watched the grief of families who finally had to admit
that some of their own had simply disappeared and would
never come home. Another of my brothers was one of these.
My mother went to her grave wondering what had become of
him. None of us ever knew.

There came a time when I could ride a horse. It wasn't easy,
not like before, and it never would be quite the same again, but
I knew I could at least take care of myself and put up a showing of respectable work. I had been thinking of Texas for a long
time. After the many years away, the delta was no longer my
home. When my grieving old mother breathed her last and we
put her under the deep black soil, nothing was left to hold me. I
made my way downriver to New Orleans like before and found
a freighter about to set sail for the Texas coast. The captain
had seen more than enough of crippled, hungry ex-soldiers, but
he decided I could earn a bunk helping the cook. I spent most
of that voyage in a hot, steaming galley. But it was worth it all
to see old Indianola materialize through the early-morning fog.
The town had grown since I had seen it that other time, but I
had no difficulty finding the place where I had slept beneath the
wharf while awaiting passage inland.

The wharves were sagging beneath the weight of cotton bales
consigned to hungry mills back East, and the ships were
unloading machinery and other goods for which Texas had
starved during the long war and the blockade that had strangled

its ports. Nobody in Texas had much solid Union coin, but they bartered cotton and tobacco and corn.

As before, I was dependent upon the generosity of people I had never seen before. Like most Confederate soldiers I had been paid little, and that in a currency no longer worth the paper it was printed on. The ship's captain gave me a few dollars for my labor, barely enough to buy a few days' meals and lodging ashore. My heavy limp and the cane I leaned upon made me a poor candidate for employment in a place where many able-bodied men hunted desperately for work. But I owned a little land near New Silesia, and I had Thomas Canfield's old promise of a job.

As before, I began looking for a freight outfit that might take me inland. I saw a line of big, heavy freight wagons near a wharf and made my way hopefully in their direction. I walked up to a man who appeared to be in charge of loading and asked where his wagons were bound. He looked me over carefully before answering. He probably guessed my situation without being told; a lot of others like me were making their way to an old home or looking for a new one.

"San Antonio," he said.

"By way of Stonehill or New Silesia?" I asked hopefully.

He frowned. "I don't remember you from Stonehill, and you don't talk none like them damned Polanders."

"I've been gone a long time," I told him.

A heavy voice spoke behind me. "I heard you mention Stonehill."

I turned and almost fell. There, staring me in the face, was Branch Isom. He carried more weight than when I had last seen him, the red beard was gone, and the lines were cut deeper into that ruddy face. But there was no mistaking the man. My hand tightened instinctively on the cane, and my first thought was that I would have to fight in another minute.

Recognition came much slower to him. I had aged a lot,

thinned a lot. But after a long moment he said, "You're Reed Sawyer."

I could only nod, waiting for the trouble to come. An angry thought flashed through my mind, that I had outlived the war only to come back here and, more than likely, end my days on the wharf at Indianola.

To my surprise he showed no enmity, no grudge over old battles. If anything, he betrayed a touch of regret. He said, "The war was not kind to you."

"Kinder than to some," I told him. "At least I'm here."

"And looking for a ride home?"

If he had forgotten our first meeting, I had not. My first treatment at his hands was something I would remember to my last day. I said, "You needn't bother about me. I'll find one." I started to turn away.

He touched my shoulder and stopped me. "We'll be rolling in a couple of hours. I'll be glad to have the company of an old friend."

"We never were friends, Branch Isom," I said.

"That was a long time ago. Things have changed. You're a soldier home from the war. I've tried to bury old enmities."

You've buried a lot of old enemies, too, I thought, but I had the judgment not to say it.

I had no wish to travel with Branch Isom, so I made a couple of excuses and worked my way down into the town, hoping I might find someone else going my way. Luck was not with me. In a couple of hours I saw the wagons moving out in a line and resigned myself to a long stay in the coast town. But a light carriage drawn by a couple of nicely matched bays came down the street. Branch Isom waved to me and pulled the horses to a stop. "Ready to travel, Sawyer?"

I had no more excuses. I had been prepared to argue that a long ride on a heavy freight wagon would probably jolt my knitting hip too much, but I could see he meant for me to ride in the carriage with him. I put old hatreds behind me in the stresses of the moment and joined the devil.

He put the bays out in front of the wagons so we would not have to eat the dust, then slowed them to a walk that would not outpace the train behind us. He wore a good suit, better than any I had seen during my short stay in Indianola. The carriage, though not new, was a symbol of some prosperity. Prosperity, I knew, had long been a stranger to most people in Texas. My first thought, a natural one in view of past history, was that he had stolen it. But again I had the judgment not to ask.

He did most of the talking. He inquired about my war experiences, and I told him in a sketchy way. I had a hundred questions I desperately wanted to ask him, but most were about the Canfields. I could not believe enough time had passed that they would be a welcome subject for him. Perhaps sensing my curiosity about his relative well-being, he volunteered to me that freighting had made him a lot of money during the war. The Union blockade had closed the Texas ports within the first months. Cotton, always one of Texas' most important money crops, had stacked up by the thousands of bales, shut out of its traditional markets. But Texan ingenuity had not allowed this condition to become permanent. Soon the bales were on their way to the Mexican border in long, dust-raising wagon trains. Carried across the border, they were sold to European buyers for gold coin or traded outright for munitions and other Confederate needs. Union ships had no authority to prevent the shipment of merchandise in and out of Mexican ports. The great wagon trains wore deep ruts into the trail to Brownsville and Matamoros. Not only had Branch Isom joined his wagons into this trade, but he had bought many more and expanded.

Isom told me, "We put a lot of cotton across that river and brought back a lot of guns and powder and equipment for you boys fighting the war. We did all we could, but I guess it wasn't enough."

It appeared to me it had been enough for *him*. Indirectly he told me as much. "I always took my payment on the Mexican side, in gold. I never did trust that paper money. People who did, like old Linden Hines, they're broke now."

"Linden Hines, broke?" That news hit me hard. Stonehill had been his town; he had started it.

"Lost his store, the freight wagons that used to haul goods for him, everything. Had a barrelful of that Richmond money when the war was over. It's not fit for wallpaper."

That hurt. I had always had a good feeling about that old man. "What does he do now?"

"Lives in the past, mostly. His daughter keeps books for me. I try to find the old man some things to do. Isn't much he *can* do, though. His health broke toward the end of the war, when he saw he was going to lose everything."

Suspiciously I asked, "Who got it?"

"First one and then another. San Antonio banks, mostly. He borrowed to keep the wagon outfits supplied, trying to help with the war. They lent paper but wanted gold back. I finally bought his store from him, but the money went to satisfy the banks."

"It's not fair if he did it all to help his country."

"Nothing is fair in this life. A man takes care of himself. Like your friend Thomas Canfield. He pulled into his hole like a badger and didn't give anything away."

That gave me the chance to ask what I had wanted to.

"He's all right? His family's all right?" I had received a few letters from Thomas' mother, early. Mail had a hard time finding me later on.

Isom's voice hardened. "Sure he's all right. Anything he ever owned, he still owns. Land-poor, maybe, without a dollar of real money to his name, but he'd eat jackrabbits before he'd borrow a dollar on one foot of that land." Isom grunted. "He can keep his land as far as I'm concerned. Give me a going business anytime, like mine . . . the town, the freight line. That's where the money is."

"Last I heard, a long time ago, Thomas and Maria had a baby girl."

Isom nodded. "She'd be three now, or maybe four. She was born after my little boy came."

I don't know why I should have been surprised at the thought of Branch Isom having children. The meanest dog can sire a litter of pups. But the thought of him bouncing a child on his knee didn't fit the image I had always carried in my mind. It was even more of a surprise, then, that he set in to telling me all about his boy. His name was James, and he was four. He could ride horseback by himself, and he could name most of the horses and mules in half of Isom's many freight teams. Once started, Isom seemed unable to stop talking about him. Somewhere in the conversation he told me Mrs. Isom had never been able to have another child. I suppose that was why Isom seemed to put so much store in this one, because there would not be another.

I kept expecting, sooner or later, that old grudges would surface in Isom's conversation, that he would turn his anger against me on the trail where nobody but his own men would see or know. But he never did. It was as though the old differences had never existed. In the few words he spoke of Thomas, I knew the angers of the past had not died, but for me personally he betrayed no resentment. Perhaps he took my army service into account, or my crippled hip, and he wiped the slate clean. All the way to Stonehill I remained uneasy, expecting trouble. It never came.

The town looked little different. Some new houses had been built. The streets were moderately busy, mostly with freight wagons engaged in the gradual renewal of normal commerce. I noticed a fair number of Mexican carts, holding their own against the *gringo* freighters. Isom seemed not even to see them. He pulled the carriage to a halt at his open double gates and watched his freight wagons enter a huge corral, all but the last one in the line. He signaled for the driver to follow him. "That

one," he said, "is for my wife. Things for the house, ordered all
the way from England. Even a piano."

Coming into Stonehill had increased my uneasiness. It had
seemed a forbidding town, especially since the death of Kirby
Canfield. Even after the many years, I still had that feeling
about it.

I said, "I'd better get down here. I'll find a way to get out to
the ranch."

Isom nodded. "You know I can't take you. Thomas Canfield
and I have not set eyes on one another in years. It is best we
keep it that way. I'd be glad to lend you a horse."

I did not want to arrive at the Canfield ranch riding a horse
that belonged to Branch Isom. I thanked him for his generosity
and assured him I would find a way. He asked me to come up
to his house and meet his wife and see his boy, James. I told
him I would, another time. He pulled away and left me in the
trailing dust, much relieved to see the last of him even though
he had shown me nothing but friendliness since Indianola. Old
suspicions die hard.

I had no idea, at first, what my next move should be. I was
not sure who I might still know here. It was in my mind that I
could seek out some of the Mexicans who had worked for or
dealt with Thomas years ago, if any still lived in Stonehill. I
started up the dusty street, one hand holding the carpetbag con-
taining nearly everything I owned, the other holding the cane
for support. I looked vainly for a familiar face.

Reading the signs, I learned that Branch Isom had his roots
sunk deeply into this town. A dramshop bore the names "Smith
& Isom" in small letters beneath the title "Texas Lady." A
blacksmith shop and livery barn proclaimed "A. Dandridge &
B. Isom." I came in a while to the big general store that had
been built by Linden Hines. The sign declared, "General Mercantile. Branch Isom, Prop."

I felt a little as I supposed the Europeans must have felt
when a usurper took the throne.

Laura Hines had remained on my mind during the long war years. I had more or less reconciled myself to the idea that there would never be anything between us except friendship, but I knew no other face that appealed to me quite so much, so I let hers be the player in many a fanciful daydream, some of a high order, some I would never have wanted her to know about. Futile or not, the dreams had been a means of lifting me out of intolerable reality and, perhaps, keeping me from losing my mind.

Isom had said she was keeping books for him. I stood in front of the store a minute, bracing up my courage, wondering how far I had let my dreams stray from truth. I had long suspected that I had made over her face to suit myself, so that the one in the dreams was probably at considerable variance with reality.

I made my way past barrels and boxes on the wooden porch and stood in the open double door, trying to accustom my eyes to the dim interior. I heard Laura before I saw her.

"Reed? Reed Sawyer?" She came out from behind a tall counter in the rear of the store. I could not see her clearly because it was dark in there, and my eyes were filling up, too. "It's me," I said.

She threw her arms around me, putting me off balance and almost causing me to fall. My hip shot through with pain, but I tried to hide it. She stood back a little to stare at me, her hands keeping a strong grip on my shoulders.

"We were afraid you were dead," she declared.

"I wrote."

"The mail service broke down, toward the last."

She made a good deal of fuss over me, which I enjoyed, but I sensed that it was friendship, nothing more. All those daydreams had served a purpose at the time, but they were dead now. I felt like crying.

She had changed a lot, or perhaps my creative memory had been at fault. She was mature, a woman well past twenty, face still pretty but eyes sad from the unhappiness she had seen. I realized we were both ten years older than when we had first met.

"You look wonderful," I said. That was true. She did, to me.

She brought herself to ask about my cane, about my thinness. I admitted that I looked as if I had barely escaped the grave, but I was sure I would get much better now that I was home.

"First thing you need is a good meal," she said. "I have the books in good shape. I'm going to take you home with me and cook you a real dinner."

I protested, but weakly. Nothing could have pleased me more.

She said, "It will do Papa good to see you. He hasn't seen much in a long time to make him smile."

I thought I knew what to expect, but seeing Linden Hines was like a blow to the stomach. He was an old man, a shell. He smiled at the sight of me, but the smile lived only a minute. He had given up the will and surrendered to infirmities that he normally might have stood off for many more years.

"I am glad you came back, Reed," he said. "So many didn't. It cost us so much . . ."

The casualties of the war had reached far beyond the battlefields.

I remembered that the old gentleman had been partial to a good toddy. While Laura was busy fixing dinner I thought I might cheer him a little. I said, "It has been a long, hard trip, and I think a drink would do me good. I would be obliged, sir, if you would go with me."

That faint smile returned. "I would be honored, sir."

Neither of us moved very fast, me burdened by my bad hip and my cane, he by his health. We went into the place called Lucky Lady, which Mr. Hines indicated was as good as any in town. Business seemed slack, but it was a time of day when most respectable people were working, if most people in Stonehill could be considered respectable. Thomas Canfield had always regarded the Hineses as something akin to Lot's family, two good people in a town of arch sinners.

We had our drinks, and I laid the coins on the bar. A voice came from the back of the room. "Keep your money, Sawyer. The drinks are on the house."

Branch Isom had entered the back door. I told him it was not necessary, but he protested that it was an occasion when a soldier came home, especially the friend of an old friend like Linden Hines. He went behind the bar, opened a door somewhere and fetched out a bottle. "This is the best I can buy, too good to sell across the bar." He poured our glasses full, and one for himself. He held up his glass in a toast: "To the soldiers of Texas, wherever they fought."

I looked closely at Mr. Hines, expecting him to betray resentment toward this man who now owned all that used to belong to him. But I saw no such emotion there. He nodded at the toast and downed the whisky and said something about its being good.

Isom said, "And now, gentlemen, I must leave you. I have pressing business all over town. Come in again, Sawyer. Mr. Hines, my compliments."

Hines thanked him for the whisky, which prompted me to do the same. I had been so surprised by Isom's generosity that I stood off balance. I could not escape a feeling that I was a calf being fattened for slaughter, though I could not imagine how.

I was not used to whisky and never held it well. It glowed like a comfortable fire in my stomach, though. Mr. Hines seemed ready to go home, so we started. He took the lead, picking his way among a group of teamsters who had just come in. They did not move aside for him. They would have, a few years earlier. My cane brought me no particular respect either. They were used to crippled ex-soldiers coming home.

From the porch down to the street was a fair distance, and I was a little slow negotiating the three steps. Mr. Hines was ahead of me, looking back to be sure I didn't slip. I heard a rumbling and a loud shout and glanced up the street. A big freight wagon was bearing down on Mr. Hines.

"Look out!" I shouted to him and tried to hurry. I caught one foot on my cane and fell down the steps. I could hear the wagon driver cursing and shouting at his mules. Through the dust and the blur of movement I sensed that Mr. Hines had stepped back quickly enough to be in the clear.

"Why don't you watch what you're doing, old man?" the driver shouted back, once the danger was past. "Damned old relics, ought not to be allowed on the street without a guardian."

I got up angry enough to do battle, even in my condition. I shouted after the driver that an old pioneer like Linden Hines was due respect, but the words were lost in the air. Nobody cared what he had been in the past. They saw only what he was now, a worn-out old man existing on others' generosity. The generosity of Branch Isom.

My conscience began nagging me. I knew all my indignation had not been over the general lack of gratitude to Linden Hines. Some was for myself. My being a wounded soldier seemed to have little meaning either; few people exhibited any gratitude. I supposed it was because we had lost the war. I had just as well have stayed home.

Laura put more steak on the table than we could eat, even with the appetite I had saved up through a long lean time. Beef was cheap, she said, even free for those who had a horse and could go get it. The war had blocked most outside markets for years. So many men had gone into Confederate service that herds went untended, unbranded. Cattle had multiplied to a point that South Texas ranges were badly overstocked, the grass short. The unbranded ran wild and free for the taking, with no one to object.

Before the war, cattle had represented wealth. Now, if anything, they were a liability.

"Eat some more," she said. "You're doing some rancher a favor."

I made the sacrifice, to my later discomfort. My thoughts returned then to the Canfield ranch. If I dallied much longer I would be obliged to stay the night. That would be an imposition on the Hineses. Their house was small and had no real place for me. I began making my excuses to leave.

Laura said, "I'll take you out there. I'll get a wagon from the company barn."

I told her I did not want to be any more burden than I had already been. Also, I had let myself become more beholden to Branch Isom than I would ever have imagined in olden times. I felt uncomfortable, owing a debt to a man like that, and I told her so.

She frowned. "That's Thomas talking, not you. Branch Isom has many faults, but he's not a completely forsaken sinner."

I figured she felt obliged to loyalty because she worked for him, and he occasionally extended cheap courtesies to her father. It struck me as unfair that Isom had enriched himself from the long conflict while soldiers like myself had paid a hard price.

Laura would not accept my refusal. I said my good-byes to her father, then walked with her to the big barn where empty freight wagons stood in a neat line and dozens of horses and mules milled in dusty corrals, pulling hay from crude racks built of mesquite. I looked around uneasily for Branch Isom, hoping not to have to belittle myself by thanking him once again. The stablemen never questioned Laura's request for a light spring wagon. I could tell she carried weight around here. One of the men confided to me, out of her hearing, that she officiated at the monthly pay table. Bought loyalty was effective, if sometimes shallow.

We rode in silence much of the time. After several years of absence I was busy taking in the country, remembering. It was drier than when I had left it, the grass poor. I could see cattle in every direction, thick as fleas on a butcher's dog.

When Laura talked it was mostly about Stonehill, which seemed to have prospered more than the average Texas town during the war because of its importance on the freighting roads. I asked about New Silesia, well remembering how nearly it had come to starvation in the beginning. She said it had suffered some harassment early because so many of the people were opposed to the war. It had not grown much but had solidified its position. Unlike Stonehill, it had been largely self-sufficient. What the Polish immigrants could not raise or make for themselves, they managed to do without. For this reason they had not suffered unduly from the collapse of the Confederate currency; they had little of it in the first place. Laura said they had broken out more fields and strengthened their hold on the little they owned. Like Thomas Canfield, they drew their strength from the land and regarded it as the only thing solid in life. Money was but sterile paper or metal. The land was alive.

When I asked about Mrs. Canfield or Maria or the two children, Laura talked easily. When she spoke of Thomas she was slower and more thoughtful, and she did not look at me. Earlier I had been tempted to ask why she had not found another good man and married him. Before we reached the ranch, I knew without asking.

Approaching the headquarters, I could see little change. There were still four houses of varying size, the double cabin for the old Mrs. Canfield, another for the Fernandez family, a small one for single hired hands, and the big frame house Thomas had built on the slope for Maria. From a distance I could see it needed paint. That, in itself, told me much about financial circumstances.

Two men were in the round bronc-breaking corral, one riding a crow-hopping young horse, the other throwing a sack under its feet to try to make it pitch. I was astounded when Laura told me these were the Fernandez boys. In my mind they should still be as young as when I had left. Now they would pass—at a distance—for grown men. But this was a country that did not tolerate childhood very long. The boys quickly tied the bronc and scaled the fence, then ran to meet us, hollering at me all the way.

It was getting to be a grim joke, everybody saying first off that they had assumed I was dead. I told them I hated to be such a disappointment. They ran ahead of us up to the big house, shouting for the Canfields to come out. The old lady was the first onto the porch. She threw up her hands and came running to meet me. She had grayed more in the nearly four years I had been gone, and the lines had cut deeper into her face, but I thought she had fared far better than Linden Hines.

Maria came out then, her brown eyes shining and beautiful. Like Laura, she had matured into a fine-looking woman. Her face was still pretty and fleshed out better than I remembered it. Her waist was fuller, the result of bearing two children, but if anything that was an improvement. Before, she had looked as if a strong wind might carry her away.

A small girl, who had to be past three now, peered shyly out from behind her, keeping one hand full of her mother's skirt, pulling it out to cover all but one big brown eye, very curious.

The two women both hugged me at the same time, while the little girl ran and threw her arms around Laura's neck, then clung to her while she looked at me with both curiosity and a little fear. Youngsters like this, growing up far out in the country, were not used to strangers. I heard the girl saying, "Aunt Laura." I saw the gentle way Laura and Maria looked at each other, and it occurred to me how unusual a friendship theirs really was.

It was a while before I knew the little girl's name. The old lady called her child, and Maria called her something I never quite understood, then or later. It was in Polish. Eventually Laura spoke of her as Katrina when the girl led her off into another room to show some doll clothes her mother had sewed from scraps.

Maria's English had improved, though she still spoke with an accent. She looked at me with pity. "We must make for you much food. We must get you fat again." I never had been given much to weight, but I realized I must look like starvation now.

Not until near dark did Thomas come home. I saw Maria's eyes light at the sound of the wagon. If I had ever doubted that he had chosen well, that look dispelled all question. The boy Kirby sat beside him on the wagon. The original spring seat was gone, replaced by a flat board that jolted the innards. The two had been shoveling stock salt into troughs at some of the watering places. The boy's rough clothing was crusted with it. He was six now, or near it, and as shy of me as the girl had been. Thomas tied off the reins and came up into the yard with a tired but happy step. The boy remained a full pace behind him and eyed me with dark suspicion. I had bounced him on my knee, but he had been too small to remember that.

Thomas stared at me a long moment without a word. He had aged more than the years alone would account for. He was not original with his first words. "Reed, I thought they had killed you," he said.

I didn't care what he said so long as there was welcome in it. He gripped my arms in the Mexican style of *abrazo;* much of his manner had come to him from the Mexicans.

I managed to say, "You told me I would always have a home here." I wondered, for by the looks of things an extra mouth might be a burden.

"I hope you never doubted that," he said.

"I probably won't be much help for a while."

He glanced at my cane but only shrugged. "You've already been a help, just coming back. Now I know things have got to get better."

One of the Fernandez boys came up, and Thomas asked him to take care of the team and wagon. He put his arm around

Maria, and they walked into the house. Laura watched them, then took the girl's hand and followed.

Only the boy and I were left. I asked, "How about it, Kirby?"

He just stood on the ground and stared in silent distrust.

I turned and went into the house alone, figuring he would open up to me after a while.

But he never did, not completely.

CHAPTER 5

The first days on the ranch produced many satisfactions, but they also held frustrations. My hip punished me for my ambition in trying to ride horseback. I went three or four miles with the Fernandez boys, thinking the pain would stop sooner or later. Instead it became so bad I had to dismount and could not climb back into the saddle. I waited in humiliation while Marco returned to headquarters and brought a wagon to fetch me home.

"You're trying too hard," Thomas admonished. "Take your time."

I said, "I was brought up to work for what I get."

Thomas' face was sad. "You're not getting much here. I haven't the money to pay you anything."

"You feed me. You give me a place to lay my head down. I owe you for that."

I owed for much more. I was not simply a hired hand, and I was not treated as one. Maria and the old Mrs. Canfield competed with each other to see who could fix the best meals for me. The little girl, Katy—Thomas would never call her Katrina—toddled after me as if I were some good uncle, even if the boy never warmed to me.

"There is a lot of work you can do in a wagon," Thomas said. "You can carry salt. You can haul supplies from New Silesia." He tried to keep my mind and my hands occupied, to make me feel useful rather than a burden, even when I knew it was not true.

I would watch him ride his favorite horse, that spirited mustang bay he called Stepper, which had never completely given up the fight and occasionally challenged Thomas' right to mastery. Thomas always won, but not without a contest. I envied him that ability and wondered how long it would be before I was a whole man again.

He asked me to go with him to San Antonio to buy goods for his struggling store in New Silesia. That store, since the collapse of Confederate currency, had become a financial tribulation to him. I sat in the lobby of a San Antonio bank and watched from a distance as Thomas humbled himself to a well-dressed Yankee banker, something I knew hurt him worse in its way than my wound had ever hurt me. He finally got most of what he had asked for, but the cost in pride was high. On the long trip home in the rough wagon, he was silent, withdrawn into a heavy shell.

When he finally spoke the suddenness of it startled me. He said, "You haven't seen your own place since you came home."

I had, one day when I was hauling salt. I had made several extra miles in an empty wagon to look upon the little piece of land I had bought with my saved wages before the war. It wasn't much, a fraction of Thomas' holdings, and it had not so much as a dugout on it for habitation. There was no point in my building one; it was too small a place to yield a living. But I felt a glow from the sense of ownership.

Thomas stopped the wagon on a knoll and gazed in silence. I could see cattle scattered across a wide, sun-baked flat and knew most of them were strays, not mine. The few cows I had owned before the war would be old mossyhorns now, the ones that might have survived.

Thomas said, "We kept up your brand for you while you were gone. We branded the increase every year."

I thanked him, though it seemed to me the work had been largely for nothing. Those cattle were worth no more than their hides and tallow would fetch, which wasn't much. And the land wasn't worth the lumber it would take to build a good house on it.

He seemed to sense what I was thinking. "Hold on to it, Reed. It will be worth a fortune to you someday. Land is the only thing that is real."

"Gold is real," I said. "This whole thing, today, wouldn't bring enough gold to plate a watch."

"Gold doesn't grow food. It doesn't keep the rain off of your head."

I spoke rashly, and immediately wished I had kept my mouth shut. "It seems to be doing very well for Branch Isom."

He shook from the impact of the name. "It will betray him someday. Through the war, when others were working for patriotism, he worked for gold. Now he puts it all back into Stonehill. He has no feeling for land; all it means to him is the roads to carry his freight wagons. That town will blow away someday, like tumbleweeds. The freight business will die with it. All his gold will be gone, and his sins will be visited on him like a plague. He will sit there with ruin all about him, but we'll have our land, Reed. The land will always be here."

We circled back by New Silesia, where he spent some time in the store with the manager Smithers, going over the ledgers. The store was like a stone weight around their necks; they had extended credit to too many people unlikely ever to pay.

While they talked about their business problems I looked over the little immigrant town. Thomas felt strong ties to it, mostly because of Maria and her people, but I was never at home there. I never had learned the language, not even enough to ask for coffee. The customs remained strange to me. Many of the Polanders had put up solid if unfancy houses—mostly of stone—in the years I had been away. I could not quite accept their way of building house and barn together, their milk stock staying in one end while the people lived in the other. I understood this was the way of the old country, but I never felt that friendly toward a cow.

Thomas was not much at going to church. Maria was faithful about it. Every Sunday she put the two children in a wagon and drove over to New Silesia. Sometimes Thomas went with her but found other things to do while she and her family and the children attended mass in the Catholic church. Other times he sent one of the Fernandez boys to make sure she had no trouble along the way. There were still people in the country who enjoyed harassing the Polanders. A couple of times, I went. The church service was alien to me, like most other things in the town. New Silesia seemed like something that had been lifted up from Europe and set down in Texas with few modifications.

We heard about the fever when it first moved up from the coast with one of Branch Isom's freighting outfits and struck in Stonehill. A Mexican wrangler told us several people in town had come down with it. Branch Isom sent his wife and young son to San Antonio to avoid their being exposed. There had been other epidemics, and none had ever touched the Canfield ranch. I remembered several times before the war that sickness had traveled inland with the freighting crews or immigrants. It would always run its course in a little while. Here and there somebody died of the fever, but people died of many other things too. Folks talk about the dangers we used to face from Indians and outlaws, but more died during epidemics in those days than ever died of arrow or bullet. Being isolated, far out in the country, was sometimes an asset. We probably missed more hazards than we realized.

One day a boy came out from town with a message from Laura Hines. The fever had struck her father suddenly, and in his weakened and spiritless condition he had died the second night.

Thomas struggled with his conscience. Not since his brother's death had he set foot in Stonehill. But the funeral of an old friend, and the bereavement of Laura, overcame his reluctance. He gave the two children into the care of Mrs. Fernandez, then four of us went to town in the wagon. Thomas hardly looked to right or left as we moved down the main street; his jaw was set in contempt for the place. Forgetting at first that Laura and her father had moved, he pulled the wagon up to the front of the large house that had long been their home. I had to tell him how to find the smaller one where they had lived since the war.

Laura was better reconciled to her loss than I expected. Maria hurried to embrace her. Laura accepted our condolences but said death had come to her father as a friend; life had lost its flavor to him.

The fever had people fearful about congregating indoors. The funeral was conducted entirely at the cemetery, a dry south wind blowing a skim of fresh earth into the open, waiting grave while the minister gave the eulogy. Maria stood on one side of Laura, Mrs. Canfield on the other, but she was strong enough; she did not need bracing up.

Branch Isom came to the funeral alone; his family was still in the comparative safety of San Antonio. He and Thomas did not speak, but their eyes met. Thomas' hatred flashed with the crackling reality of St. Elmo's fire. Isom quickly looked away. The uneasy truce of recent times had not overcome the open hostility of other years.

When the service was over Isom made his obligatory comments to Laura about the loss of a good man, the father of the town. Thomas watched him resentfully as he walked away.

"By rights he should not have come here," he said. "He robbed Mr. Hines of all he owned, even the will to live."

Laura shook her head, her voice quiet but firm. "Branch Isom did not cause our trouble. That came because Papa gave everything he had to the cause he believed in. Isom just picked up the pieces."

"He could afford to. He hadn't given anything away."

Thomas seemed to realize the subject was painful to Laura, so he fell silent. But he watched Isom while the man's buggy was in sight.

Maria tried to persuade Laura to go to the ranch a few days, to get away from the unhappy town and the sorrow it had caused her. Laura shook her head. "I've fallen behind on the books. What I need most right now is work to keep my mind busy."

We followed her home but found a goodly number of sympathetic women there. She would not lack for company. Thomas made excuses, and we left. He was relieved to put the town behind him. On the way home, nobody talked much. Mrs. Canfield finally began to comment upon the fever, and how fortunate we were to live in the open country where God kept the air clean.

Her words were ironic, for Thomas' mother was struck down a few days later. No one knew much about the fever or its causes. We could only guess that she had caught it somehow at the funeral. Thomas immediately asked me to take the children to Maria's people in New Silesia. So far the fever had not struck that town. Little Katy did not mind; I had already seen how much she loved her grandparents. But the boy Kirby was silent during the wagon trip to the Polish town. His eyes were resentful when I turned him over to the old couple. He understood what they said to him in their language, but he stubbornly refused to answer them except in English. I sensed that I had been introduced to a shameful secret. Even as the Brozeks fawned over the children, it was easy to see they were covering up their hurt. Kirby came to the door of the stone house and watched me as I left for the ranch. He said not a word, but I felt his eyes following me.

Unlike Linden Hines, Mrs. Canfield had a strong wish to live. She put up a battle that she seemed for a time to be winning. But it was not enough. The doctor managed to see her only once, for he had more than enough suffering patients in

Stonehill. Maria stayed beside the old lady constantly during
the three days and nights she struggled. She was still on her
feet, but barely, when the fever carried Mrs. Canfield away.
Thomas just sat in his mother's rocking chair at the foot of the
bed and stared. He did not talk; he did not weep. He just sat
there, rocking.

Maria cried a little, then put that behind her and tried to
comfort her husband. She seemed unable to reach him, and her
silent eyes pleaded to me for help.

I said to Thomas, "I'll go to the preacher. Your mother was
a believing woman. She'd want the words read over her."

A quick nod was the only sign that he had heard.

I knew without asking that he would want to bury her up on
the slope, alongside his father and brother. Backing away, I
said, "I'd better fetch the children home. They ought to see her
laid to rest."

He stopped rocking. "No, there's fever here." That was all
he said. He started rocking again.

Maria followed me to the porch, tears shining in her eyes.
"He does not let me help him," she said.

I told her, "He's not a man who leans on people. He stands
by himself." It struck me how thin and haggard she looked. She
had slept little the last several days. "You'd better help yourself," I said. "You'd better get some rest."

She nodded, but she would not do it, not so long as she
thought Thomas might need her.

The minister was almost as busy as the doctor. There had
been other deaths since that of Linden Hines. He promised to
come out to the ranch as soon as he could, but all preparations
had to be made ahead, for he could not stay long. I tried to
think of any people in town who should be notified. The only
friend Mrs. Canfield had there, so far as I knew, was Laura
Hines. Laura put a few clothes together and rode back to the
ranch with me in the wagon.

Scarcely a dozen people stood at the graveside to hear the

brief services. Thomas said little. He stood alone. When Maria reached once for his hand, he pulled it away and folded his arms.

I glanced at Laura. She frowned.

Laura did not like the tired, drawn look on Maria's face, and she offered to stay a day or two. Maria insisted she was all right; a good night's sleep was all she needed. Thomas took no part in the conversation. He seemed not even to hear it, though he was only an arm's length away. He responded to nothing until Laura said, "If you will then, Reed, please take me back to Stonehill."

The word "Stonehill" seemed to bring Thomas around. "You should get away from that place, Laura. It brings nothing but misfortune and death."

She gave him a look of surprise, as if not quite believing he cared that much for her welfare. "I have nowhere else to go."

It was in my mind—I had not given up—that someday *I* might provide her a place to go, when I was able to build my land holdings and my cattle herd some more, and after I put up a house of my own. But the thought passed when we sat in the wagon together. She glanced back, and what I saw in her eyes for Thomas, I feared I would never see there for me.

Maria started to climb the steps as we pulled away. She never made it to the top. I saw her sway, then fall. Laura cried at me to stop. She was down from the wagon and running before I could bring the team to a halt. I saw fear strike Thomas. He called Maria's name as he knelt and tried to lift her to her feet.

By the time I got the team still and the reins wrapped around a spoke, Thomas had Maria in his arms and was rushing into the house with her. Laura was directly behind him. I followed them into the bedroom, where Thomas gently placed Maria on their big hand-carved wooden bed.

"She's just tired out," he said desperately, more to himself than to the rest of us. He was trying to believe it, but it was obvious he did not.

Laura felt of Maria's hand and then her forehead. "It's more than that." Fear came into her face. She immediately took over, for Thomas seemed helpless, as he had been helpless when his mother was burning with fever. This was an enemy he did not know how to fight.

"Reed," she commanded, "run down and fetch Mrs. Fernandez. Then hurry to town and drag that doctor out here; bring him with a gun if you have to. Thomas, you help me get these clothes off of Maria."

Thomas had braced his feet, and he stood like an ox struck behind the horns with the flat side of an ax. Laura saw he was stunned. She gripped his shoulders and shook him savagely. "Thomas!" I waited in the door until he began to respond, then I ran down to the little Fernandez house.

What Laura said about bringing the doctor with a gun if necessary was not much of an exaggeration. He still had about all he could do without leaving town. I thought I would have to wrestle his hefty wife, who protested that *he* would be the next to die if he didn't get some rest. I sympathized with both of them, but I had to sympathize with Maria more. I took him to the ranch.

Nobody had to tell me the situation was grave. The hard-set look in Thomas' eyes said that, and the quiet desperation of Laura. Maria was talking irrationally, crying out in words I could not understand about things that had happened long before, or perhaps never happened at all.

I looked to Thomas to see if I could do anything for him. He seemed unaware of me, even when I spoke to him. Laura touched my arm and beckoned me into the parlor. Quietly, her voice trembling, she said, "You'd better hurry to New Silesia and bring her parents here. You'd best not lose any time."

"They have the children. I shouldn't bring the children to this fever."

"There's other family to leave the children with. But bring her parents, and hurry."

I never had been able to converse with the Brozeks very well because of the language problem. I went directly to the church and found the priest hunched over a giant Bible. I explained the situation. He went with me to the Brozeks'. Katy was playing in the front yard of the rock house with some other children, chattering happily in Polish. Kirby was off to himself, chunking rocks at some chickens. The girl recognized me and came running, shouting my name. Kirby walked only partway to meet me, then stopped, saying nothing. I could tell he hoped I had come to take him home, but he was too proud to ask, or to seem eager. He had much of Thomas in him.

Anguish came into the old couple's faces as the priest told them of my message. Kirby listened in silence. I could tell he understood it all. Katy cried and begged to be taken to her mother. The old grandmother picked her up and smothered her in her arms and hurried outside to call to a neighbor. In a few minutes she had the children placed with others of the family. The priest had a buggy, more comfortable than the ranch wagon, so he took the old folks in it while I followed close behind, one of Maria's brothers riding with me. The long miles I had made, first to Stonehill and then to New Silesia, began to tell on me, and the brother took over the reins. I tried to nap sitting up, but the wagon was too rough. I sat with my eyes shut and kept seeing all those anguished faces.

We arrived almost too late. Maria opened her eyes at the sound of voices. She recognized her parents and called their names and cried out for her children. Laura tried to explain that they had stayed behind to protect them from the fever, but I don't think Maria understood. She sank back into the fever. When the priest leaned over her with his beads and began to give her absolution, I knew the ordeal was nearly done. She cried out once and was gone.

The old couple crossed themselves and leaned into each

other's arms. Mrs. Fernandez made the same sign and turned her face into a corner. I looked into Laura's tired, stricken face, then to Thomas, frozen, unseeing. His mind had carried him far away, denying reality, rejecting recognition of death. For several minutes he did not move. Then he gripped Maria's shoulders and tried to shake her awake.

"Maria! Maria!" he cried.

Laura gently touched his arm. "She can't hear you, Thomas," she whispered.

He shook Maria harder and kept calling to her. When realization finally reached him he pushed to his feet and stared down at that silent face now without pain. A terrible look came into his eyes, the look that had always frightened me a little. Instinctively I glanced at his hip, though I realized he was not carrying a gun. The dark thought came to me that if he had, he might use it on himself.

He spoke to no one, looked at no one, but turned and strode out of the room. The fear still pressed on me, so I followed him, keeping my distance. I thought it unnatural that a man could go through so much and never cry. I had not seen him cry when he buried his brother Kirby, or his mother. I saw not one tear in his eyes now. He walked carefully down the steps and toward the barn. Quietly I followed fifteen or twenty steps behind him, not sure what he might do or what I *could* do. He stopped at the horse corral.

His bay mustang Stepper was in there, pulling hay from a rack. He turned his head to watch Thomas, and he made a nervous, rolling noise in that long, ugly nose. Thomas walked in, shutting the gate behind him. I kept my distance, moving up quietly and looking between the poles. Thomas walked slowly toward the horse, his hand extended. The bay watched him suspiciously, little ears flicking in nervousness. Once he started to turn and run away, but something in Thomas' manner seemed to hold him. The bay flinched as Thomas reached out and touched his neck. Thomas slipped his left arm under the neck and up the off side. He patted the horse a while. If he said anything, it was in a whisper I could not hear. Then he had both arms around the horse's strong neck, his face buried in the dark mane, and Thomas did something I had never seen him do. He cried.

The horse, normally nervous as a cat, stood quiet and still, as if it understood, and let Thomas spill out all his grief.

I walked back to the house. The best help I could give Thomas was simply to leave him alone.

Thomas Canfield had long seemed a man the world could not touch, a man too strong to bend before the wind. Now, for a while, the fight was gone out of him. He held his ground on just one thing. Maria's parents wanted to take her to New Silesia for burial in consecrated ground. Thomas insisted she would be buried in the family cemetery up on the slope. That, too, he said, was consecrated ground, hallowed by so many he had loved. The priest blessed the place, and it was all right.

Beyond that one issue, he had no strength left. If the denizens of Stonehill had come then to drive off every head of cattle and to post a confiscation notice on his land, I do not believe he would have resisted. He drew into a shell where nothing from outside could reach him.

The girl Katy was too young to realize fully the meaning of death. Kirby knew. I never saw him cry, but I could see the pain and the helpless anger in his eyes. He did not know who to blame, so he blamed everyone. Some of the anger was directed toward his father for sending him away and some toward me for taking him. During the services I saw him resist attempts of Maria's parents to hold his hand. He stood alone, as his father stood alone.

The worst part of all was in returning to that big house, which must have seemed empty to the children. Thomas brought Mrs. Fernandez up from her own little place to live in the house and be a guardian of sorts. Her own sons were doing man's work if not drawing a man's pay. They slept in the little house where they had grown up, though they went to the big house to take their meals, cooked by their mother for them and for what was left of the Canfields. Much of the time they were not at headquarters anyway; they were often camped on one part of the ranch or another, looking after the cattle, batching. So, for that matter, was I. My hip had healed to the point that riding horseback no longer hurt me much, unless I let the work carry me too far into the night. I still had a limit.

I saw more of Kirby than of his sister because Thomas made it a point to keep the boy with him as much as he could. Where he went, Kirby usually rode by his side, on horseback or in the wagon. They talked little to each other. At least, Kirby talked little. His father volunteered points to him about the cattle or the horses, about the wild animals they encountered, about the land itself. Kirby absorbed this teaching without much comment. The long months went by, but he remained as distant as the day his mother was buried.

Despite our isolation, we heard things. Business began picking itself up from the floor where the lost war had left it. Union dollars, though still scarce, began to sift into the channels of commerce. Thomas had stubbornly held onto his ailing little store in New Silesia, not so much for its own sake as for the irritating competition it could give to Stonehill and to Branch Isom. Somehow he managed to pay off some loans and get himself back into reasonably good graces with the bankers in San Antonio, themselves hard put to find much real U.S. specie in circulation. An awful lot of scrip and plain old-fashioned barter were used in those days.

I had a horse in my string called Stomper, a name well given. He had a way of walking and trotting that jarred a rider's innards. Every time I rode him my hip would ache, but I could ill afford *not* to ride him, for a horse unused tends to forget his teaching and backslide into outlawry. I could have turned him over to one of the Fernandez boys, but they had not done anything to me that justified so sorry a treatment. I kept the horse as penance for whatever shortcomings I might have in the sight of the Lord.

One afternoon the pain was so sharp that I quit early and rode back toward the house while the sun was still an hour or so high. I cut into the Stonehill road and heard somebody hail me. I stopped Stomper and turned him around, welcoming a chance to shift my weight in the saddle and perhaps ease the aching hip.

The rider who trotted to catch up to me was one I would recognize from a mile away. Branch Isom.

Thinking back, I could not remember ever seeing him on the Canfield ranch. I saw no pistol on his hip, though he carried a rifle in a scabbard beneath his leg. Everybody did; that was no sign of war.

He reined up and offered a few pleasantries. His manner was cordial enough that my initial suspicions were suspended, if not dismissed. He seemed no longer the unrepentant sinner that he had appeared years before, when we had first made our acquaintance. Perhaps it was the graying with the red in his hair, or the deeper lines in a ruddy face growing heavy with the weight of years and relative prosperity. He seemed to have mellowed. Or perhaps I had seen so much brutality in the war that he paled by contrast.

He spoke of regret for the sorrows that had befallen the Canfields. He said, "I'll admit I never felt any love for Thomas, and it's certain he's had none for me. But I've had only the kindest thoughts for his womenfolks, even that Polander girl he married."

That surprised me a little. I felt honor-bound to ask about his own family. He said they were fine; his wife and son had waited in San Antonio for the fever to run its course. "Boy's getting to be a goer. I'd like to have brought him, but I didn't know what kind of reception I might get from Canfield. Some things a boy shouldn't see or hear."

It wasn't any of my business, but I felt compelled to ask anyway. "What have you come to see Thomas for?"

"Business. A mutual profit for both him and me, I hope."

My suspicions revived, though not so strong as before. It had been a long time since much good had come to this place from Stonehill, Laura Hines being the exception. She had visited occasionally on Sundays to look in on the children, or so she said.

I rode into headquarters with him. He told me much I had not heard about the Union occupation army and Indian troubles farther west, and of business trends and hopes and fears. As we approached the barn I saw Thomas' wagon in front of the salt house. He was shoveling salt to carry to the watering places. Kirby stood in the wagon bed, evening out the load with a shovel whose handle was longer than he was tall.

"Thomas," I called, "you have company."

His jaw dropped and his face darkened as he recognized Branch Isom. He cut his eyes reproachfully to me as if Isom's visit had been my doing. "Isom," he said. Not *welcome* or anything like that. Just "Isom." Recognition, but not approval.

Isom studied him a long moment before he said a word. Then he laid most of it right out on the table. "Thomas Canfield, you've never liked me, and I've never liked you. Men have been killed over differences smaller than we've had. But that's all in the past."

Thomas said nothing.

Isom said, "I have a business proposition. It could be profitable to both of us."

Thomas let his suspicions come bitterly to the surface. "More profitable for you than for me, I would warrant."

"Quite possibly," Isom admitted. "But I would carry considerable risk. Your profit would be guaranteed."

Thomas noticed his son watching Isom with unusual interest. Curtly he said, "Kirby, you go to the house."

Kirby was hesitant, and Thomas told him again, his voice brooking no question. "Go!" Kirby went reluctantly.

Thomas never invited Isom to step down from the saddle, so Isom sat there. He said, "Thomas, they're building a railroad west into Kansas."

Thomas pondered that fact a moment and failed to see significance in it. "You should not have to worry about that. They can't hurt you until they build one west from Indianola to San Antonio. Then you may be selling your freight wagons cheap."

Isom passed over the sarcasm and explained that the new railroad was opening up a market for beef in the East. "Cattle can be sold at the railheads to be shipped back there."

"We're a long way from Kansas. What good does that do us?"

"Cattle have legs. They can be walked to Kansas. I have started putting together a herd to take north. I'll buy cattle from you here and take all the responsibility and all the gamble. I'll pay you two-and-a-half a head for whatever cattle I can use. You won't have to go anywhere or take any risk. It's cash money, Union silver, placed into your hands right here at your corrals."

Thomas looked down, hiding his eyes. "What will you get for them, up in Kansas?"

"I won't lie to you. There is every indication they could bring fifteen dollars, perhaps more. But it's a long way and a risky trip. I'll lose some on the way. I *could* lose them all. If I make it, I'll earn a good profit. If I don't, I'll stand a loss. In either case, you'll have your money before the cattle ever leave this place."

Thomas said, "You've never handled cattle."

"I've handled horses and mules for years." He paused. "It's cash money. I'll bet you haven't seen two hundred dollars in Union specie since the war."

Thomas stared off into the distance, toward the slope where he had buried so many Canfields. When he turned I could tell from his expression pretty much what he was going to say. He would have dealt with Lucifer before he would deal with Branch Isom.

Coldly he said, "Isom, you were right when you rode up here. You never liked me, and I never liked you. What's between us is not forgotten. It never will be. I would not do business with you for a hundred thousand in Yankee gold."

Isom's face flashed to anger. I saw at least a little of the hostile Isom I remembered. "That's your final say?"

Thomas nodded grimly.

Isom had as much pride, in his way, as Thomas. He would not argue or plead. He said only, "I had hoped we could bury the past."

Thomas grunted. "Not until they bury *me*."

Isom's shoulders were stiff as he rode away. Thomas watched him as if half expecting him to turn and come back shooting. There had been a time, once, when that might have happened.

I could contain myself no longer. "If he offered you two-and-a-half outright, you could probably have carried him up to three. Maybe even three-and-a-half."

Thomas turned his back on me.

Next morning, without any word to me of what he planned, he left for San Antonio. Late the second evening he returned with two men following him in a buggy. One was a San Antonio businessman wearing a light duster over a good suit. The other was obviously a cowman by his clothes, his boots, his Mexican-style hat. He had the look of a man who had spent his life in the sun. Thomas introduced them as Mr. Jensen and Mr. Hayes.

"I have agreed to sell these gentlemen two hundred cattle at two dollars a head," he said.

I shook their hands and tried to look pleasant, though I quickly calculated that this represented a clear loss of one hundred dollars from Isom's offer.

Hatred could be expensive.

Branch Isom was by no means the only person putting cattle together for the trail to Kansas. These men had the same
notion, Jensen putting up the money and Hayes the ability. Before the war Hayes had trailed cattle all the way to Missouri,
and during the war he had taken some over into Louisiana to
feed the Confederate soldiers. He had the look of a man who
knew what the cow was about to think before she had time to
think it. Those old cowmen bore a mark hard to explain but
easy to recognize.

Thomas had us round up cattle from the end of the ranch
nearest to Stonehill. Many people in town had become accustomed to helping themselves to Canfield beef. Thomas had
done nothing about it because the cattle had been worth little
anyway. Now times appeared to be changing. Thinning the cattle nearest to town might not stop the beef killing, but it made
the thieves work harder. Hayes and Jensen were not interested
in cows. A cow-calf herd was slow and difficult to trail. Anyway,
the Yankees wanted beef, not breeding animals. The range was
overstocked with long-aged steers and unbranded bulls born
during the war years. They belonged to whoever caught them, if
they bore no brand. As we gathered cattle, the two buyers were
joined at headquarters by a crew of hungry-looking cowboys
excited about the chance for a paying job that would put real
silver in their pockets for the first time since the war.

Thomas had never been one to talk much, and he had said
less in the time since Maria's death. He had shown little real interest in anything other than those two children. Now he spent
a lot of time with Hayes, listening to all the old cowman volunteered to tell him about driving cattle. When the counting was
over and the cowboys left with the herd, Thomas had a canvas
sack that clanked with the heavy sound of silver.

"Sounds like more than it is," I remarked, remembering that
he could have gotten better payment from Branch Isom.

"The devil always outbids the righteous," he replied, looking
oddly satisfied as he watched the dust stirred by the departing

cattle. "Reed, I want you to get an early start in the morning. Ride over west and see if the Ramirez boys want three or four months of work." They were among the men who used to go with us mustang hunting. "Get Abe Johnson and Farley Good and the Martinez brothers. We'll need a good crew who know cattle and horses."

"To do what?"

I could see something kindling in his eyes, a fire I hadn't seen there in a long time, a touch of excitement I had feared had died forever. "To put our own trail herd together and drive them to Kansas." He hefted the bag of silver. "This will be enough to outfit us."

I stood there with my mouth hanging open, thinking of a dozen good objections but undecided which to voice first. I didn't want to dim that light growing in his eyes.

Thomas said, "If their cattle can walk that far, so can ours. If they can get fifteen dollars at the railroad, so can we."

I said, "Branch Isom will throw a fit."

That, I realized, was one of the factors which put that new spirit in Thomas' face; that thought had come to him days ago.

"Yes," he said with satisfaction. "He will."

CHAPTER 6

My circle took me two days. I brought some of the men with me. Others were to follow when they could put personal business in order. Seeing some of those faces again made me remember old mustang-running days, and I felt a chill as the dark face of Bustamante came into my mind. It was said he had gone down into Mexico and had been killed fighting on the side of the *Juaristas*. Yet, there were among the Mexicans some who swore they had come across him in the brush country, in one secret camp or another. Somehow, people never wanted to let any of the old outlaws die; they kept seeing them whether they were dead or not.

I took the Fernandez boys and the crew that had come with me and started putting cattle together. Following Hayes's advice and example, we sorted out steers and bulls and hazed them toward headquarters, pushing cows and calves back out of the way. We had no fenced pastures, so we kept a couple of riders circling the outside, preventing the gathered cattle from drifting far.

Thomas arrived with a couple of extra *gringo* cowboys and a Mexican cook he had come across in San Antonio. They brought two well-used wagons, one with high sides built for hauling freight, the other an old canvas-covered army ambulance, wrecked and partially rebuilt. The words "U. S. Army" had been painted over but still showed. The heavy wagon was full of food and supplies. The ambulance was empty.

I watched little Katy rush out of the house and down the

steps to throw her arms around her father's neck. Kirby kept his reserve.

Thomas took for granted what had been done in his absence; he had expected no less. I watched the youngsters go reluctantly back up the steps as Mrs. Fernandez called them to supper. Thomas lagged behind.

I said, "It's going to be tough on them, you being gone three or four months."

"They'll go with us," he replied. "We'll fix bunks in the old ambulance for them and Mrs. Fernandez."

I had never been inclined to give Thomas advice, but I could not accept this without argument. "We can't take those kids."

He didn't even look at me. "I wasn't much older than Kirby when we left Tennessee."

"That was another time. They'd be better off here at home with Mrs. Fernandez. Or with Maria's folks over in New Silesia."

"They're *my* children. I won't leave them with anybody." His eyes cut at me, telling me the argument was finished.

Laura Hines came out the next Sunday to see the children. Her reaction was the same as mine. Thomas' decision remained as stern. "I know of no one I'd leave them with."

She thought on it a little. "Leave them with me."

He wavered, for a moment. That idea had not occurred to him. "You couldn't stay with them and work too."

"I can keep books anywhere. I can do it at home."

"At home in Stonehill?" He spoke the name with bitterness. The moment of wavering was past. "That town has brought grief to this family ever since it began."

"This trip could bring a lot more." She looked accusingly at me. "Why haven't you talked him out of this?"

"I tried." Nothing more needed to be said.

Laura spent longer than usual with her Sunday afternoon good-byes. She held to the girl, her eyes begging Thomas. "Katy, at least."

"They're my children," he said, ungiving. "They're my responsibility."

Thomas avoided a similar argument with Maria's parents by simply not letting them know of his plan until too late. The first day's drive carried us to New Silesia and a little beyond. Thomas departed the drive long enough to take the ambulance and Mrs. Fernandez and the children into the little Polish town. He left me in charge of the herd, so I did not see or hear whatever challenge they gave him. But when we camped on water at dark, Thomas rode up with the ambulance. The look on his face spoke of victory hard won.

Those were the earliest days of trail driving north. Trailing was still an instinct, not a science. The first drives had no clear pattern to follow, so each outfit felt its way along. Later, old drovers would look back and laugh at the mistakes we made and the time we occasionally wasted. What most of us did, at first, was simply to use what we knew of handling cattle on the open range. We knew little of lead steers, of proper pace, of avoiding stray cattle, of always being sure where the water was, of crossing strange and unfriendly rivers. We did not even have a proper chuck wagon. That was a refinement yet to come, credited to cowman Charles Goodnight and copied and altered to fit the fancy of every trail boss and herd owner who pointed their cattle north. We simply carried grub and cooking utensils in the bed of the old freight wagon Thomas had brought from San Antonio. A certain amount of it had to be unpacked and then repacked at every meal, which soon had us wishing for a better way. The invention of the chuck-box was inevitable, with its drop-down lid that became a work table for the cook. But we didn't have it on that trip. We did the best we could with what we had, hoping for better the next time. If there was to be a next time.

We pushed the cattle hard the first few days to keep them tired, less likely to spook and run, or to try to turn back south toward home. The cattle were half wild, many of the bulls dragged out of the brush and handled by men and horses for the first time in their lives. They were always looking for something to booger at, and they often found it. Those first three or four days they must have run at least twice a day. Usually it was in the wrong direction, so the distance they made was wasted. I never could understand why cattle had such an adverse way of stampeding every direction except north.

The wildest of the early runs was on the third day, not long after we had strung them out in the morning. A black cloud had been hanging low in the north since long before daylight. We had watched a distant flashing and knew the cloud was coming at us. After sunrise, thunder rolled from west to east like the sound of cattle running. A sharp clap put the herd into a panic, running past the swing men on the east. We spurred as hard as we could push our horses, for the ambulance with the kids and Mrs. Fernandez was in the path of those cattle.

Mrs. Fernandez was not one to lose her head in a crisis; she had seen a fair number in her time. She swung the team to put the vehicle into an easterly direction, same as the cattle were running. This would keep it from being struck broadside. The cattle broke and went around either side of the ambulance. A few bumped it going by, but no real damage was done. The worst that happened was that one of the mules got its forelegs over the wagon tongue and hung up in the harness. Kirby was hanging out over the front, watching, and the jolt bounced him off of the wagon. He jumped to his feet, waving his hat and shouting. The last of the cattle swung away from him.

Thomas had been on the far side of the herd, so he was one of the last to reach the ambulance. I saw that everything was all right with Mrs. Fernandez and the kids, so I waved the rest of the riders after the cattle. Thomas spurred up, slid his horse to a stop and hit the ground running. His face almost white, he grabbed Kirby into his arms and hugged him. I thought the boy was in more danger of being crushed by his father than he had been from those running cattle.

Mrs. Fernandez's face was pinched. Katy tried hard not to burst into tears. I turned to Thomas. "I can keep the herd moving. Why don't you take the kids back to New Silesia? You can catch up to us in a couple or three days."

He just gave me that look. "You never give up, do you?" he asked.

I saw in his eyes that he would not change his mind. "I do when I can see there's no use fighting it anymore."

If Thomas did not change, little Kirby began to. Looking back on it afterward, I suspected it might have begun when he managed to wave the last running cattle around and escaped unhurt from a bad situation. He began to develop an attitude that nothing could hurt him if he stood his ground, an attitude to which he had been amply exposed at home. Thomas could not watch him all the time. When his father was not nearby, Kirby would saddle a horse and leave the ambulance to ride with the herd. Thomas soon gave up forbidding him. He ordered Kirby to stay with the drags at the rear of the herd where nothing was likely to happen to him. In no time Kirby would move up to the swing position and often to the lead, where one of the older, more responsible men was riding point. He accepted no authority except his father's, and that only when Thomas was nearby. No one else could send the boy back where he belonged. If one of the hands became insistent, Kirby would tell him in either English or Spanish to mind his own business.

He took to sleeping on the ground at night with the rest of the crew. A wagon, he declared, was for women and girls. Only on rainy nights would he compromise his pride and go into the covered ambulance. As the days wore into weeks he settled into a position with or near the Fernandez boys during days, and he rolled his blankets near theirs at night. The other men had started the drive mostly as strangers to him, and grown men at that. He never warmed to them much.

Kirby seemed to avoid Thomas as much as he could, pulling

away on his horse when Thomas approached. I took it as a natural thing, a youngster's desire to escape his father's critical eye and reprimands for his shortcomings. But Thomas took it for something more. Nights, sometimes, I would see him staring at his son across the campfire, his eyes troubled.

One day we came to a small creek that under normal circumstances would be no challenge. Rain had fallen during the night. It must have been heavier upstream, because the creek was rushing along at a goodly clip. Thomas motioned me up to the point, where we sat with Farley Good and studied the brownish water, colored by the soil the rain had carried into it. We quickly decided it didn't present much danger to the herd. I could have thrown a rock across it with a sore arm.

"Put them into the water at a run," Thomas said, "and they'll be over before they know they're wet." He looked back, seeking out the Fernandez boys. Wherever they were, there Kirby would be also. "I'm putting Kirby in the ambulance."

I became too busy rushing cattle across to pay attention to what was happening behind me. By and by I heard a boyish whoop and saw Kirby spur his pony into the stream. I yelled at him to come back, but the order was lost in the noise of the cattle splashing into the swollen creek. Halfway across, the pony lost its footing and turned under. Juan Fernandez hit the water before I had time even to move. I went in behind him.

Kirby came up threshing. Almost as he surfaced, Juan grabbed him, pinning him against his leg as he carried him out of the creek and onto the far bank. I was beside him the last few feet, ready to grab if Juan showed sign of losing his hold.

I was too scared to talk, and Juan looked as if all the blood had drained from his face. But Kirby was laughing.

I struggled to say something. Juan gave Kirby a strong shaking. "Your papa say you don't come on your pony. He say you ride the ambulance."

"I didn't get hurt," Kirby said defensively. "And neither did my pony. Looky yonder, he's coming out of the water. Go get him for me, Juanito."

"I get a *belt* for you," Juan said angrily.

Thomas rode up, his eyes afire. "Go catch his pony, Juan. I've got the belt for him." He stepped from his saddle and caught Kirby as Juan let him slide to the ground. Thomas unbuckled his belt and pulled it from his trousers, then held it at half swing. Kirby drew himself up to take the blow, jutting his jaw but not quite closing his eyes. He stared defiantly at his father. I sat on my horse, watching the conflict play itself out in Thomas' face. Slowly he lowered the belt without using it on his son.

In later years he *would* strike him. By then it was too late.

Sharply he said, "Next time I tell you something, you listen."

Kirby did not reply. He stood braced, still half expecting the belt to strike, but he yielded nothing.

"Damn it, boy . . ." Thomas said slowly, not finishing what was on his mind. Juan brought up the dripping pony. "Get on him," Thomas commanded Kirby, "and then you stay on this side of the creek. Don't you go back into that water for anything."

It was an empty order. There was no reason for Kirby or anybody else to cross that creek twice. But Thomas had to assert his authority, even if he had lost it.

Most trail drives were a long, slow stretch of boredom, with a few minutes of excitement now and again to take the place of the sleep there never was enough time for. Crossing rivers was one of the few times we had any reason to let our blood pump fast, once the herd wore the "run" out of its system. A few cattle naturally took the leadership, rising up off of the bedgrounds at daylight and setting out to graze. About all we did was point their direction, north. Most of the other cattle would gradually get up and fall into the positions their natures best suited them to. Like people, cattle developed a standing in the social order. The ones highest up protected their places with all the jealousy of a San Antonio matron. The ones which took the lead in the first days of the drive held it the rest of the way. The ones which fell back early stayed back. After a time you would get to know the individual cattle and just where they belonged on the drive. Unless one went lame or sick, he would not vary his position much.

After the first days, when the cattle were used to walking and Thomas was sure Branch Isom hadn't started his drive yet, we let the Longhorns graze along and set a pace that suited them. Thomas occasionally dropped back a few miles to be sure nobody was catching up to us with another herd. He became touchy about our front position; he would not stand for pressure from behind. One day we saw dust way to the rear, and I went with Thomas to see about it. Another herd was pushing along at a pace faster than ours. I thought for a while it might come to a fight. Thomas held on to that lead like it was a gift from the Almighty, and anybody who challenged us was on the devil's string. Hot words passed, but the trail boss of that other outfit shrank back from the look in Thomas' eyes. He decided his herd needed a day of rest to make up for the hard pace it had traveled.

The nearest we came to a genuine scare was with the Indians. They had been in the back of my mind from the beginning because there was no way to get to Kansas from South Texas without crossing Indian land. I had always felt we were overdue for trouble in the old days when we ran mustangs in the wild country far to the west of Stonehill, but somehow we had never run into them. Now we were pushing through country the government had granted to them, and a herd of cattle was a hard thing to hide. The people who had been north ahead of us said the Indians wouldn't usually bother an outfit that let them have a few cattle, but this was never a sure thing. A lot of them hadn't settled yet and hadn't agreed to any reservation. You couldn't tell by looking whether they were treaty Indians or the wild bunch. If they took a disliking to you it didn't make much difference anyway, people said.

I was riding point the afternoon they came on us, out of the sun. In the first excited moment I thought there must be fifty, but later I recounted and found only seventeen. I guess it was always that way with Indians; there were seldom as many as there seemed to be. They made no warlike signs against us, but they all carried armament—bows, lances, a few old muskets worn out before they traded for or stole them. They stopped in a ragged line. One who made it clear he was the leader came toward me, walking his horse. He held up one hand to show he was peaceful, but I watched the other hand more; it held a rifle with a barrel four feet long. He started talking and making signs with his hands. I decided he had rather talk to us than fight us, though he might fight if the talk ran thin.

Thomas loped up to me, some of the other men just behind him. The ambulance had stopped. The two Fernandez boys had moved beside it, ready to protect their mother and the kids.

My first thought was that Thomas' sign language would be no better than mine, but I didn't consider the fact that he had been married to a Polander woman and had talked to both her and her family with his hands. It didn't take him and the Indian but a minute or two to find enough common ground that they could parley.

Thomas' face was cold serious. He told me, "He says he's got a lot of hungry people. He wants a beef for every man he brought with him."

By this time I had made the count and told Thomas how many that was, in case he had not counted for himself. He agreed with me that this was a San Antonio fancy-house price. He bargained awhile and cut the number to ten. The Indian looked satisfied; I suspected he had been willing to settle for less.

We had been so taken up with the Indians that the sound of the wagon chains right behind us came as a shock. I turned in the saddle and saw that Mrs. Fernandez had brought up the ambulance. I suppose she didn't consider her boys protection enough; people instinctively looked to Thomas for that. Kirby had his horse up real close to the ambulance, and real close to Marco and Juan. Little Katy stood behind the wagon seat, beneath the tarp cover, but she looked out around Mrs. Fernandez, her eyes as big as brown saucers.

The Indian stared at her, and a smile spread across his face. That took me completely off balance; I had never featured Indians smiling at all. He edged his pony up closer to the ambulance. It shied at the wind-flapping canvas, but he held it with a tight rein. Katy faded back under the cover, where we could see little more than her eyes.

The Indian motioned for her to come back out. I suppose he was trying to tell her he intended her no harm, but Katy was not interested in getting better acquainted. The chief laughed and turned to Thomas. Thomas was trying not to show his uneasiness, but the effort strained him. His hand was on his gun butt. The Indian made some more sign talk. Thomas gradually eased, but he contrived to work his horse around between the Indian and the ambulance.

"Katy," he said, "he wants to trade for you. He says he'll give us six ponies."

In later years Katy would laugh over it, but at that moment she did not laugh. Her fear gave way to a flash of anger.

"You're not going to do it, are you, Papa?"

He said, "Six ponies is a lot."

She leaned out from under the canvas, a long steel pothook gripped in both of her little hands. "I'll hit him on the head!"

The Indian broke into laughter. He turned back to the men behind him, pointed and said something about the girl. I knew he was approving of the fight he saw in her. Several of the Indians laughed, which only deepened Katy's anger. Thomas held out his hand to calm her.

"It's all right, girl. He didn't mean it. Nobody meant it."

The chief turned away from the jesting and back to business. He signaled a few of his men forward. They rode into the herd with him and started picking some of the fleshier cattle. The deal had been ten. I decided Indians didn't count very well, because they took an even dozen. But Thomas didn't count, either. As soon as the Indians were on their way he climbed down from his horse and into the ambulance to hold the girl in his arms.

When it was over, Thomas was shaken more than Katy. Kirby didn't have much to say that night, but he had stood his ground too.

Backing down had been bred out of the Canfield line.

We saw Indians only a couple of times after that, and just once that they actually approached us. Mrs. Fernandez kept the ambulance way back—Thomas had a long parley with her about that. Katy crouched down behind the canvas with the pothook in her hand, out of sight until the Indians had taken a few steers and were gone beyond the hill. I kept watch on Kirby out of the corner of my eye. He stayed by the Fernandez boys, who stuck to the ambulance like burrs. That night Kirby had more to say. He was bolder, now that he had experienced Indians close up for a second time without coming to harm. He talked about what he would have done if the Indians had made any threat. The Fernandez boys pestered and hoorawed him about his bragging until he started hitting Marco. They were friends again, after a while, but Kirby could flare like a match.

We made all the river crossings with a certain nervousness, mostly because of the kids and Mrs. Fernandez. Rainstorms, hail, wind—all these things visited our drive and left us miserable, though they did not strike anywhere near the heart. We reached the railroad tired and thinner than when we had started in Texas, but we had lost no men and relatively few cattle.

The railroad was something new to most of the Texans, though I had seen a few in the war. That first train clanging and banging and smoking up a black cloud awed some of our crew.

It came near stampeding the cattle. Both of Mrs. Fernandez's boys had to hold tight to the reins to keep the ambulance team from running away. The wagon team ran a little and bounced off some of the bedrolls.

Ours was one of the early herds. We were considerably ahead of the season's rush, when several herds might hit the shipping pens the same day. Most of our crew was primed to ride into town and paint it a bold shade of red, but Thomas stood tough. Nobody was to leave the herd until it was sold and delivered. I heard some grumbling, but Thomas did not.

Selling the cattle would have been easy except for Thomas. Three or four prospective buyers rode out to the herd where we held it on a flat above town. Each new one raised the bid a little. Thomas waited until he had a bid from every buyer, then told the high bidder he wanted payment in gold. That gentleman turned three shades of crimson and declared that his check was as solid as the U.S. mint. Thomas calmly told him he knew nothing about the mint, but he was familiar with the value of gold. Mr. High Bidder denounced him as an unreconstructed rebel and rode off talking to himself.

Thomas sold the cattle to a man who had bid him a dollar a head less, but he said it was better to lose a dollar than to risk it all to fraud. The buyer was friendly enough, a former Yankee major named Thorne, who had his beard cut in the style of Ulysses S. Grant and wore a black coat even though it was summertime. He chewed a foul black cigar that refused to stay lit. Unlike some other people we ran into in Kansas, he knew the war was over, and he didn't throw it in our faces that we had been on the losing side.

"I'll have to send to Chicago for the gold," he said.

Thomas told him, "We spent three months getting here. We can wait."

The buyer smiled. "I can't blame you for wanting gold. They've thrown out the honest men in Washington and turned the treasury over to blackguards. It would surprise me none at all one day to be able to buy their paper money at ten cents on the dollar."

Some of the men itched for a frolic, but Thomas was as ungiving as an army sergeant. We loose-herded the cattle, watering them a bunch at a time in a natural lake that held water from the spring rains. Not a man in the crew got to drink anything stronger than Mrs. Fernandez's coffee, which she boiled with sugar in it. The enforced sobriety didn't bother me; I had been in the army long enough to work that foolishness out of my system. But some of these younger fellows had never been out of Texas, so even the lamp-lit windows of a little Kansas prairie town looked like Chicago. They thought they had seen the elephant.

They never got a chance to test it. The gold arrived with the same engine that fetched a string of empty cattle cars to haul away the herd. We eased the cattle up to the stockpens and counted off a carload at a time. The engine chuffed and smoked, pulling the cars forward a notch each time we finished loading one and sealing its sliding doors.

I caught the distrust in Thomas' face as the train finally left, smoking slowly eastward up those shining tracks. But the Yankee major was an honest man. I accompanied Thomas inside the bank while the crew waited restlessly outside. Thomas and the major each counted out the gold coins on a table in a small side office while I stood at the door with a nervous deputy marshal who was sweating over his responsibility.

Thomas closed and strapped a pair of new saddlebags he had bought to carry the money. The major said, "I would suggest you lock it in the bank's safe until you are ready to leave town."

The deputy's jaw dropped. But Thomas relieved him of worry. He said, "We guarded the cattle. We'll guard the money." His fingers closed so tightly over the bags that his big knuckles showed dots of white. I saw something in his eyes not unlike the look men sometimes get from drinking too much. It was not the money itself which intoxicated him; it was the thought of the land he could buy with that Union gold. Money was a tool, like a pick or a shovel. *Land* was what counted.

The men still waited outside. Thomas told the major, "I promised the crew a drink when the business was all done. I would be pleased if you would join us."

"It would be my pleasure, if you will allow me to buy a round."

Thomas frowned at the men. "Just one. I need them sober."

The bartender pulled a pair of bottles up from beneath the plain bar as we walked in. He saw the major and put those bottles back, taking better ones from in front of the big mirror behind the bar. He started pouring the glasses full. Thomas stared dubiously at the two Fernandez boys, then held up a finger. "Just one," he told them. The first round was Thomas'. We were sipping the major's round and looking at our trail-beaten images in the long mirror when we heard several horses. In a minute boots were stamping off dust on the little porch. Three dusty, bearded Texans walked through the door. One of them took two steps and stopped.

Thomas pushed away from the bar and dropped the leather saddlebags to the floor, freeing his hands. He made no move toward his pistol, but he was ready.

I stared a moment before I recognized Branch Isom, but Thomas had known him at a glance. Isom had the wearied look of a long, hard trail, his red-and-gray beard untended, his clothes hanging in ribbons, his boots crusted in dried mud. Resentment rose in his eyes, then he shoved it away.

"Congratulations, Thomas," he said evenly. "You got here ahead of me."

"That was my intention."

"I never regarded it as a contest."

"It has always been a contest between us, Isom."

"It seems so, but I can't remember anymore why it ever started."

"I remember."

The men with Isom were strangers. They appeared as bewildered as the major. Isom told them, "I believe we will be more comfortable elsewhere."

Everybody stood in silence until Isom and his men were gone. The major seemed disconcerted, being drawn into a situation he knew nothing about. In all likelihood he would be called upon to bid on Isom's herd after being made to appear in league with Isom's enemy.

Thomas said, "We have things to do. We'll take leave of this town in a little while."

The major shook Thomas' hand. It was clear he thought leaving was a good idea. The men in the crew, by and large, would not have agreed, but they had not been asked.

As we rode toward camp I moved close to Thomas. I said, "You owe these men a night free in town."

Thomas shook his head. "I owe them wages, nothing else."

He had an effective way of shutting off argument simply by not listening anymore. We brought the wagon up to a mercantile store and loaded it with supplies for the trip home. Thomas had sold the extra horses, leaving us just the ones we rode and a few to meet any happenstance. Thomas would not brook much in the way of happenstance.

We were able to travel only a couple of hours before evening. It seemed to me we could just as well have waited until morning, but we put that many miles between ourselves and the temptations of the town and camped with a crew dissatisfied but sober. I had thought Thomas would ease a little as we headed south, toward home. But he was just as tense carrying the money as he had been driving the cattle.

I said, "If it'll make you feel better, we can set a guard over the camp." The men had been used to night guard on the way up. Thomas shook his head. "I won't sleep much anyway."

I hadn't been asleep long when I was jarred out of it by somebody hollering, out in the night.

"Hello the camp," he called. "I'm coming in."

I threw back my blanket and grabbed first for my pistol, then for my boots, which was all I had taken off.

Thomas shouted, "Who's out there?"

"Major Thorne," came the answer. "Is that you, Canfield?"

"It's me. Come on in." Thomas held a rifle.

The major was alone. The fire had burned down so that it did not throw much light on him, but he was easily recognized by the military set of his shoulders. His voice was urgent. "You had better rouse your camp, Canfield. I am not the only company you are going to have tonight."

There was no handshaking or attempt at pleasantries.

Thomas demanded, "What is the trouble?"

"Word has reached me that a gang of toughs is going to raid you for your gold."

Thomas spat. "Branch Isom!"

"No, not Isom. Some of the riffraff that have been hanging around town to see what they can steal from better men's labor. The whole town knows I paid you in gold."

Thomas was silent a minute, staring at the old ambulance. "This is as good a place as any to defend ourselves. But we have to get those children out of here, and Mrs. Fernandez."

We had crossed a dry wash just before we stopped for the night. We had ridden up onto higher ground to make camp, a standard precaution in country where a quick rain somewhere else could bring a rush of water down on a place that hadn't seen a drop. I suggested we hide the woman and children somewhere in that wash, where no stray bullets would find them.

Thomas agonized over it. "I don't want to be separated from Kirby and Katy."

"They could be killed if they stay here," I told him.

He called the Fernandez boys to him. "I want you-all to take

your mother and Kirby and Katy and hide out in the wash yonder. Go far enough to be out of the way."

Katy did not want to leave. Kirby kept his silence. Thomas
hugged the girl and handed her to Mrs. Fernandez, saying,
"Take her and go, quick." The Mexican woman carried Katy
while Kirby walked behind her, looking back at us with regret.
The Fernandez boys each carried a rifle.

Thomas turned to the major. "I thank you, sir, for coming to
tell us. Now I believe it is time you leave this place."

"I would stay and help."

"You've helped already. You have no stake in this, and there
is no need for you to risk your life. I have good men here, all
sober."

The major was an honest man with a good heart, but he was
not rash. Extending his hand, he said, "Good luck," and rode
off, making a wide swing away from the trail to avoid an un-
pleasant midnight meeting.

I had had military experience, but Thomas did not ask me
for advice. He ordered that the horses be moved into a little
grove that was like a black patch in the moonlight, a couple of
hundred yards away. We tied them there, hoping they would be
far enough from gunfire not to hurt themselves surging against
the ropes. That done, we pulled back a little way from camp,
from the ambulance and the wagon, leaving our bedrolls.
Thomas carried the saddlebags over his shoulder. He spread us
in a semicircle, covering the camp from the southeast so that no
fire would be directed toward the kids.

We were prepared for a long and nervous wait, but they did
not give us that much time. Almost as soon as we were posi-
tioned, we heard the soft plodding of hoofs to the north. The
riders were walking their mounts, trying to make no noise, but
a horse is not by his nature the most silent of animals. He rolls
his nose, his stomach sloshes of water, and the more conten-
tious will squeal and bite if a strange horse gets too near. For a
while we could only hear them, then we began to see them, a

vague dark mass moving slowly toward us in the thin moon-light. They drew close together as they spotted the two vehicles, or perhaps the dying light of the campfire. Some of the horses stamped nervously, but the men were evidently talking in whispers.

Suddenly they came spurring, fanning out to hit the camp broadside. Gunfire flashed in the darkness, roaring and ringing in our ears as the riders fired into our blankets, into the wagon. When one of them put three quick shots into the ambulance, Thomas came up from the ground with a curse and began firing his rifle. In a second or two we were all shooting. The surprised raiders shouted and screamed and fired back, but all they had to shoot at was the flashing of our guns. That, in the night, was half blinding, working against our marksmanship as well as theirs. The black powder burned our noses and put us to chok-ing, the way I remembered it from the war. It brought up all the old feelings I had known of fear and hate and exultation, mixed up together and confusing.

Amid the fire and smoke and milling of frightened horses, we could not see much, but neither could they. Two or three men rode over and past us. One of them fell, crying out to God for mercy. The thought struck me that God hadn't sent him on this errand.

As suddenly as they had come, they were gone, the ones still on horseback. As best I could tell, half a dozen rode away. A couple more escaped afoot, limping and carrying themselves hunched over in pain.

None of us left our places at first, each waiting for somebody else to move. The black smoke still clung thick and heavy, catching in our throats, burning our eyes. I saw men on the ground where our camp had been. Some moved, some didn't. Three horses were down, kicking and fighting and squealing.

Thomas was the first to move in. He walked warily, hunched over to present less of a target. He stopped to shoot one of the wounded horses, and I thought for a bad moment he was going to shoot a wounded man who lay nearby. The raider pleaded for his life. Thomas picked up a pistol, then poked his way among the other fallen men, kicking weapons from their reach. A couple of the men were beyond using them. Thomas shot the other two horses, putting them out of their pain.

We counted two men dead, another far into his dying. Three more were wounded but not in immediate danger unless Thomas lost his head and shot them. I could see the temptation rising in him.

"You," he seethed to a man sitting on the ground, gripping a bleeding leg, "you fired into the ambulance. If my kids had been in there you'd have killed them!"

"I didn't," the man pleaded, feeling death's cold breath. "I didn't shoot in there. God as my witness."

Thomas couldn't really have told one man from another, dark as it was, the gunflashes blinding us. He just fastened onto that man because he was available and seemed a little less shot up than the others.

Thomas demanded, "Where's Branch Isom?"

The man sobbed, "I don't know no Branch Isom."

"You're a liar!" Thomas shoved the muzzle of his pistol against the bridge of the man's nose. "Branch Isom led you out here."

The man was crying so that he could not answer. Thomas took that for answer enough, but I didn't. I said, "We've got no solid reason to think Branch Isom was behind this. The major told you himself it was a bunch of the town trash."

"It has the smell of Branch Isom," Thomas insisted. "He would have killed my kids!"

I was convinced he was wrong, but it was a waste of time and breath to argue with him. He wanted so badly for it to be Isom that he would ignore any contrary evidence. If I had ever doubted how deeply his hatred had gripped him, I knew it that night.

A voice called from the darkness. "Hello the camp."

Thomas replied, "Come on in, Major."

Major Thorne dismounted. The smell of smoke and blood had his horse dancing in nervousness. The major made no idle comments and asked no empty questions. He could see the wounded and dead for himself. "How many hurt in your party?"

"None seriously," Thomas told him. "We have you to thank for that."

The major said, "I couldn't bring myself to ride far. I saw what was left of them tearing off for town. I knew you'd bloodied them."

Thomas stood beside the ambulance, poking his finger at the bullet holes in the canvas. His anger had not lessened. "If my children had been in there . . ." It seemed to strike him for the first time that the two youngsters and the Fernandez family were still in the wash, probably frantic to know what had happened.

"Reed," he said, "you and the men get up the horses and hitch the teams. We'll leave as soon as I fetch the kids." He started for the wash, trotting hard.

Thomas never had actually asked if any of us were hurt. He had seen everybody, and nobody was down. I did some quick checking and found one of the cowboys had taken a shallow bullet-burn along his hip. It did more damage to his clothes than to his body. We had the teams harnessed and the horses saddled by the time Thomas came back, carrying Katy. Kirby followed. Thomas turned the girl so she would not see the wounded and the dead. He quickly lifted her into the ambulance. Kirby stared at the carnage.

Thomas roared at him, "Boy, you get yourself into that ambulance." Kirby did not move fast enough to suit him, so Thomas grabbed him by one arm and the seat of his britches, hoisting him up.

The major said, "You're going back to town, aren't you? The law will want to know all about this."

Thomas' voice was bitter. "Where was the law tonight? If they want to talk to us they can come to Texas."

"What about these wounded men?" the major asked. "They could die if you just leave them here."

"Then let them die. Good-bye to you, Major." Thomas swung into his saddle and waved his arm. We pulled away from that unlucky camp, leaving three wounded men crying for us to help them. Thomas acted as if he never heard, but I did. I kept hearing them for years.

CHAPTER 7

We traveled fast and hard the first two or three days, pushing until the teams were plainly giving out. Thomas looked back often. I thought at first he was apprehensive over possible pursuit, but that was not it. Toward the end of the first day he told me, "I didn't want to leave that place, Reed. If we hadn't had the children with us I would have ridden back into that town and faced up to Branch Isom and had it out with him for once and for all."

I tried to tell him again that I did not believe Isom had anything to do with the raid on us. He just rode off and left me. He never wasted time on things he did not want to hear.

He was not given much to talk, and he talked even less than usual as we picked our way south the way we had come. We met many trail herds pushing north, but we stayed on the upwind side and visited little. I would catch him rough-counting the cattle and mumbling to himself as he figured up how much money they might bring at the railroad. It was unlikely many would receive as much per head as ours; the market would go down as the season went on and the numbers increased. The fact that we reached the market ahead of him probably cost Branch Isom a dollar or two per head.

We were bone-weary as we moved into the familiar rolling country that meant home was just ahead of us. The sight of those South Texas prairies and occasional tangles of thorny chaparral was as welcome as a mother's face. We skirted around New Silesia. Thomas did not offer to explain, but I supposed he did not want Maria's folks to see the kids so trail-gritty and tired. He would clean them up and feed them up, *then* show them to their grandparents.

We came in sight of the homeplace, the houses, the barns, the corrals and fields. I sighed in relief. "I don't think I will ever leave again. This is one trip I never want to repeat."

"You will," Thomas said matter-of-factly. "There is money to be made taking cattle to the railroad, money to be invested in land. You'll make the trip again, and so will I."

I could think of a dozen arguments. The best one was in the ambulance, tailing up the outfit. "But the kids . . ."

"I made a mistake, taking them. I realized it the day Kirby nearly drowned. It was too late then. I'll rectify that mistake now."

He did not explain himself, and I did not ask him.

I never could understand how news could carry so fast. The morning after we reached home, Laura Hines arrived in a buggy, pulling right up to the big house. Katy shouted and ran down the steps. The woman and the little girl embraced one another and cried. Thomas and I watched from the barn, then walked up to the house. Kirby stood on the porch, looking at Laura but not running to her as his sister had done. Laura had to go up the steps to him. She tried to hold him, but he struggled away.

Thomas stopped at the gate and studied the woman with his children. I could not be so calm. I still thought Laura Hines was the finest-looking woman I had ever seen. I wanted to take hold of her but could not bring myself to do it. I shoved my hand forward. She hugged me. I melted to a mixture of delight and despair.

"It's good to have you back, Reed." She looked past me toward Thomas. "All of you. I haven't had a night's sleep the whole time, worrying about these children." She stepped back from me and put her hands lovingly on Katy's shoulders. "I'll bet you have a lot of stories to tell me."

Katy said, "An Indian wanted to buy me, but Papa wanted too many ponies."

Laura looked reproachfully at me. "You took these children where there were Indians?"

Kirby could not let Katy's story go unchallenged.

"Aw, it was just a big joke. Those Indians were scared of us."

Laura turned toward Thomas, watching him as he slowly came up onto the porch. The reproach drained swiftly from her eyes.

"Welcome home, Thomas."

"Hello, Laura. I'm glad you came out. I was going to send for you."

They did not hug; they did not even shake hands. They just looked at one another. Thomas reached for the screen door and held it open. "Come in, Laura. We have things to talk about."

He closed the door behind them, leaving me with the two youngsters on the porch. Katy went inside, but I heard Thomas say something to her, and she came out again, disappointed.

I said, "You-all haven't seen the colts. You'll be surprised how much they've grown while we were away." They followed me to the barn, and I kept them busy.

After a long time Laura came out looking for us. Her face was flushed. She was trying to hold down excitement. "Children, your father wants you at the house."

Kirby was brushing one of the colts and did not want to leave. He paid no attention to Laura. I told him sternly, "You go up yonder and see what your daddy wants." Katy had not waited; she had gone on ahead.

Laura stayed, trembling a little. I could not tell whether she wanted to laugh or cry, but she was holding back one or the other. She blurted, "He asked me to marry him."

I felt as if I had been kicked in the stomach. I knew upon reflection that this should not have come as any surprise. Badly as I wanted her myself, she had never had eyes for any man except Thomas Canfield.

I asked a foolish question. "What did you tell him?"

"I told him I would."

It took me a while to work up the nerve to ask the next question. "Do you think he loves you?"

Tears edged into her eyes. "He was honest with me, Reed. He likes me. He respects me. But the only woman he ever loved lies on that hill yonder." She pointed her chin toward the family cemetery.

"Then why . . ." I started.

She cut me off. "He needs a mother for those children. The trail drive was a nightmare because of them. He wants to know they'll always be here safe, with somebody who cares for them."

"Katy cares for you, too. But I don't know about Kirby."

"I'll have to manage with Kirby. He'll learn. We'll both learn."

I was suddenly angry at Thomas, angry because it seemed to me he was buying Laura much the way he would buy cattle or horses or a block of land. "So Thomas gets a mother for his children. What do *you* get out of this?"

"A home. *His* home. I'll be near him from now on."

"Near him, but not really *with* him. Will that be enough for you?"

"It's more than I've had."

I slapped the palm of my hand against a post so hard that it hurt. "You can't be happy with half a marriage."

"Happier than I've been with none at all."

Over the years I had learned to tell from Thomas' eyes when an argument was over. I saw that look in Laura's. I took her hand and said, "I've never said anything to you, but I think you know how I've always felt."

"I know. Sometimes I've wished it could be otherwise for me, but it never will."

"Then, be happy, Laura."

"I will," she said. She kissed me and returned to the house.

The wedding was quiet, almost as if Thomas did not care to have it noticed. As usual he did not explain himself. Laura told me he felt that a show was inappropriate because it had not been so long since Maria had died. She did not have to tell me the rest, the fact that this was a marriage of convenience on his part, almost a business arrangement, done for the children rather than for himself. One did not throw a public celebration over the buying of property.

A handful of us, close friends all, watched the ceremony in the parlor of the house Thomas had built for Maria. He was solemn, almost regretful. Laura glowed. Kirby, young though he was, saw through it about as well as any of us. After the vows had been spoken he walked onto the porch by himself and stared darkly up the hill toward the cemetery. Katy went out after a minute. I followed them because I felt like a hypocrite, joining the other people in telling Thomas and Laura how fine a match they were, how everybody knew they would both be very happy.

Katy was puzzled by her brother's coldness. "Aren't you glad we've got a new mother?"

He turned on her in a flash of anger. "We don't have a new mother. She's just going to watch after us, is all. Mrs. Fernandez could have done that."

He walked out to the barn and proceeded to soil his new suit chunking rocks at the milkpen calves.

Looking back, it is hard to pinpoint just when Kirby started going wrong. At times I remember the river crossing on the drive to Kansas, but the seed may have been planted earlier. It might even have been there from birth, an inheritance of the wild anger which sometimes cropped out in Thomas. I was gone a lot of the time and did not fully realize the extent of Kirby's rebellion until later.

After the wedding I made up my mind I did not want to live at the headquarters anymore, so near Laura. Of course I could not give Thomas my real reason, so I told him I had decided it was time to put up a house on my own land and see after my own interests. If he saw through me he gave no indication of it. He said, "I have been making some plans, Reed, and I was counting on you to help me with them. We can make money supplying cattle to the railroad market."

"I don't want to go back up that trail, not this soon."

"You won't have to. I can hire other people to do that. I want you to travel around the country buying cattle for me and shaping up herds for the trail. You have a knack for that kind of thing. You have an easy way of dealing with people, something I never learned."

I couldn't deny that. Thomas had just one way of dealing with people, on his own terms. If they didn't like those terms, there was no compromise, no deal.

When I still hesitated, he said, "You'll be my full partner in the operation. Whatever we make, half of it is yours. You can buy a lot of land."

I found that I enjoyed traveling. Over the next several weeks I saw a great deal of South Texas, visited a lot of ranches and became acquainted with a large number of people. It was my observation then, and still is, that as a class the people who make their living directly off of the land are among the most honest there are, probably because the land itself does not compromise or accept excuses. A person can lie to his fellow man and even to himself, but he cannot lie to or cheat the land. If he does not irrigate her with the proper amount of sweat, she will not produce for him. She will not be short-changed.

We put together three more herds in time to go up the trail that season, using the money received for the first herd at the railroad. Not many people in South Texas had any clear idea what cattle were worth up north, so prices hadn't increased much. They were glad to get rid of some surplus and lay their hands on real Yankee gold. Most trades in the outlying parts of the state were still by barter, and these people had little to barter other than cattle. They would gladly trade several steers for a barrel of flour or a sack of coffee beans. Poverty lay like a curse across the land in those first years after the war. Nobody had much, and a lot of people had nothing.

Once I unexpectedly met head-on with Branch Isom at a salt-grass ranch not far from the steamy Gulf of Mexico. Usually I was ahead of him, offering better prices and getting the better cattle. He wound up having to take a lot of the aged steers and the staggy kinds castrated too late in their lives. These too would fetch a price at the railroad, but not like the three- and four-year-old steers that could gain weight on a slow drive and arrive at the railroad in flesh enough for slaughter.

Isom and I sort of circled each other, wary as town dogs encountering a stranger. We shook hands and then stood apart, awkward and both wishing we were somewhere else. He said, "You've been busy, Reed Sawyer. Most places I go, you've been there and left."

"I don't plan it that way," I said.

He half smiled. "It would please Thomas Canfield if you did."

I didn't try to deny that. Isom frowned. "I heard he was blaming me for that robbery attempt up in Kansas. I want you to know, Reed, I had nothing to do with that."

"I never thought you did."

"But *he's* convinced I did, so the hell with him. He's a little bit crazy, I think."

I had never considered Thomas in quite so extreme a light. I changed the subject. "How's your family?"

"Fine, just fine. Got my boy with me out in the buckboard. Bet you haven't seen him in a long time. Come on out and let him say howdy to you."

I really wasn't wanting all that much familiarity, but I couldn't with any kind of courtesy turn him down. I followed

Isom to his buckboard in the shade of a big moss-hung liveoak tree. "James," he said to the boy, "I want you to shake hands with Mr. Sawyer."

The boy was about Kirby's age, probably already taking some schooling. He had a bright, eager look about him, like a boy who would learn well because he wanted to. He looked me in the eye when he shook my hand; most youngsters won't do that without coaching. Kirby wouldn't; he never had. I glanced at Branch Isom and saw the strong pride in his round, reddish face. Whatever he might have been once, he was a father now. He did not have to tell me he was wrapped up in that boy; it showed all over him.

Isom said to his son, "Mr. Sawyer has beaten us here, James. I expect we'll have to go somewhere else."

I could see partisanship rise in the boy's eyes. I could not help thinking of Kirby, if he and Thomas had been in the same situation. Kirby probably wouldn't have given a damn.

I found myself asking, "Son, you really want these cattle here?"

The boy said firmly, "My daddy does."

I said, "Then your daddy will get the chance to make the first bid on them." Later, when Isom made that bid, I didn't raise it. I rode away from there wondering what Thomas would say if he ever heard what I had done. I wasn't going to tell him. It would have been worth going through the storm, though, just for the pleased look I saw on that boy's face when his father got the cattle he wanted.

Thomas was always a man to keep his promises, but occasionally things worked out so that he could not. He was unable to find anybody he thought was suitable to boss that third and last set of cattle up the trail. I had to do it myself. The snow was starting to fly a little by the time I sold the cattle at the tail end of the season's market and turned south, carrying Thomas' saddlebags heavy with gold coin. The raw north wind helped hasten my trip home, that and the memory of the robbery attempt the spring before.

I never told Thomas that Branch Isom and I pooled our trail outfits and rode back to South Texas together for mutual protection. Because some of the Canfield crew as well as his came from Stonehill, I remained with him until I watched his arrival at home, his little boy James running out onto the porch, then down the tall steps and into the yard to throw his arms around his father. Isom carried the boy up onto the porch where his wife waited, and Isom hugged both of them.

He had not made nearly so much money out of the trail season as Thomas and I had, but it seemed to me he was rich in one respect that neither Thomas nor I would ever be.

I turned loose the last of the crew and rode to the ranch alone, reining up in front of the big house a while before dark. I tied my horse to the fence, unstrapped the heavy saddlebags and walked wearily up the steps, thinking surely someone must have seen me.

Katy had. She flung open the door and shouted, "Uncle Reed." I received, in a distant-relative sort of way, the kind of greeting Branch Isom had gotten in town. Laura came into the hallway at the sound of Katy's shout. To a tired and lonely man she looked beautiful. I wanted to crush her, but I reached out my hand and took off my dusty old hat.

She shook my hand. "It's good to have you back, Reed."

Kirby appeared at the end of the hall. He stared at me with no more emotion than if I had been some stranger come to sell his father a load of hay.

"Where's Thomas?" I asked her.

Sadness showed in her eyes before she covered it. "Mr. Canfield is off looking at some land west of here. He had no clear idea when you'd be back."

Mr. Canfield. "He's gone a lot, I suppose."

"He works awfully hard."

I slid the saddlebags from my shoulder. "I'd best put this in

the safe." Thomas had bought one in San Antonio after the first
trip. It was in the parlor, where some people would have placed
a piano.

Laura watched me close the safe and give the knob a turn.
"You must be starved."

I told her I would eat at the bunkhouse. We had a full-time
Mexican cook there now for the growing number of cowhands.
Mrs. Fernandez had been relieved of all responsibilities other
than the care and feeding of her sons Marco and Juan. But
Laura would not hear of my going. She insisted I needed and
deserved a good woman-cooked meal, served on a table with
real dishes instead of tinware. After all that time on the trail I
could put up no good argument.

By this time I had the use of the old double log cabin where
Thomas' mother had lived so long. I cleaned up and put on
some fresh clothes and made my way back to the big house
with mixed feelings. Being that close to Laura was both pleasure and pain.

Katy was helping Laura in the kitchen, happily fetching and
carrying. There had always been this free and happy and loving
relationship between them. I did not see the boy. In a bit the
table was set and ready. Laura stepped into the hall and called
for Kirby. He did not come. Katy kept her head down when
Laura asked her if she knew where her brother was. Reluctantly the girl said, "He went to the barn."

"I told him not to. He knew supper was almost ready."

Katy flushed a little, clearly wanting to defend her brother
but knowing he was in the wrong. I said, "I'll fetch him."

I found him sitting on a mesquite-rail fence, studying a mare
and a newly-born colt. I said, "Your supper's ready."

He ignored me. I said, "Come on, son, before you get yourself in trouble. Your mother wants you."

He turned on me angrily. "She's not my mother. I don't have
to do what she says."

Never having raised any kids of my own I didn't know how

to answer that. I had a strong inclination to exercise my hand about six inches below the back of his belt. I just reached up and plucked him from the fence, took his hand and led him to the house. He pulled back on me all the way. He ate his supper in grim silence, pushed his chair away from the table and stomped off to his room. I tried not to look at Laura.

Katy said, "I'll tell Papa. He'll spank him."

Laura shook her head. "Don't tattle. We'll have to find a way to handle Kirby ourselves, you and I."

I asked her as gently as I could, "This happen much?"

She only nodded. I asked, "Does Thomas know?"

She nodded again. "He's done all he knows to do."

I thought I knew something but tried to keep the idea from showing. I guess she read my mind. She smiled uneasily. "He's tried that. He's tried love too. I guess the only thing that will work is time."

She was wrong about that. Time made him worse. He soon hit that period when he was growing rapidly, and all of it away from Laura and Thomas. By then Thomas had twenty-five or thirty cowhands scattered over the place, ranging from devout Christians to devout hellions. Kirby seemed, when he had the choice, to tag after the hellions.

When he was eight I caught him smoking tobacco swiped from somebody in the bunkhouse. When he was ten I found him slumped against a corral post in a stupor, an empty whisky bottle on the ground. I never told Laura or Thomas; they had enough worries.

I didn't enter the big house oftener than was necessary anymore. Remembering the warmth and happiness there in Maria's time, I found the place cool. From the beginning, Thomas had formed the habit of addressing Laura as Mrs. Canfield, and he was Mr. Canfield to her. The relationship was one of formality and respect on his part. On hers there was always a holding back, a love suppressed out of fear that it would be rebuffed. Only with Katy did Laura let herself go. She lavished on the girl all the affection she wanted to give her husband and step-son. Had she lived, Maria could hardly have been much closer to that flashing-eyed child.

That seemed only to widen the distance between Kirby and the rest of the family.

Katy was always eager to visit her grandparents in New Silesia, and Laura seemed happy to take her. Whatever reservations the old folks might have had about seeing their daughter's place in the house taken by someone else, they accepted Laura as a friend. The difference in language was always a problem, but Katy acted as interpreter; she spent enough time in New Silesia that she spoke Polish as well as she did English.

Kirby was another matter. He seemed always to have something he had rather do than visit his grandparents. At first I thought it might be simply that he did not want to ride in the buggy with his sister and stepmother, that he thought it unmanly. I offered to take him there myself. I had just as well suggest that he shovel out the corrals.

"They're just dumb old potato-eaters," he declared. "I don't want to see them."

If he had been mine I would have struck him across the mouth. Kirby glared, daring me. I might have done it had I not heard Thomas behind me, cold as December. He had been in the barn. He had a look in his eyes that usually meant blood to somebody. "Reed," he said very quietly, "I want to have some words with my son."

Badly as Kirby needed correction, I dreaded what that look bespoke.

"Thomas," I argued, "he doesn't know what he's saying. He's been listening to foolish talk from men who ought to be fired off of this place."

There had been more and more of those lately, men who laughed at the Polanders and condemned the Mexicans.

Thomas' voice took on an extra barb. "Go somewhere, Reed."

I went somewhere, but not so far that I didn't hear the crackle of heavy leather striking against cotton britches. Kirby did not cry.

His feeling against his grandparents seemed only to deepen; it was as if he blamed them for his punishment.

When he was about fourteen Kirby started running with the Hallcomb boys. Their father was a muleskinner by trade and had been fired by just about every freighting outfit from San Antonio to the Gulf. During one of his periods between jobs he was in the Alamo city helping create a boom in the saloon business when a prominent merchant was pistol-whipped one dark evening and the receipts of a busy Saturday removed from his safe. The crime was never solved. Some people thought it strange that old Goodson Hallcomb showed up back in Stonehill soon afterward with enough money to buy a little stockfarm. In those days you didn't throw accusations around unless you had the facts. Nowadays they'll sue you for slander. Back then they were more likely to come looking for you with a pistol.

Hallcomb was good at raising and training draft stock for the same freight outfits that had fired him, and the San Antonio merchant soon made back all he had lost in the robbery, so most people abided by the old adage and let a sleeping dog lie. They wished he did as well at raising his boys as at raising and training mules, though. They were a salty pair, Bo about a year older than Kirby and Speck two years older. They were frecklefaced, tobacco-chewing, knot-fisted and knot-headed. Besides mules, old Goodson raised a crop of corn every year, part to feed and part to drink. Growing up, those boys of his put away more of the old man's corn whisky than of milk.

Thomas warned Kirby to stay away from that unholy clan, which made him turn to them all the more. At first it was mostly harmless things like riding the old man's wild mules. That led to drunken sprees in which they turned over farm outhouses and let pigs out of their pens into people's gardens and bobbed off the tails of some choice buggy teams.

Thomas was inclined to severe lectures and now and then a strong application of razor strop while Kirby leaned over the washstand by the back porch of the big house. It was always a case of punishment but never of correction. In no time Kirby would be back with the Hallcomb boys, dreaming up some new form of devilment for the community.

One Sunday Kirby and the Hallcombs, well supplied with the old man's corn, rode into New Silesia and fired at the church bell while mass was in progress. Then they tried to ride their horses into the church itself, to the shame of Kirby's old grandparents. Katy happened to be with the Brozeks. She pulled her brother out of the saddle, no hard chore in view of his condition. She then pounded him over the head with her grandmother's old-country Bible, which weighed almost too much for Mrs. Brozek to carry.

Kirby was shamed more by his sister's publicly administered retribution than by the words of the priest, who led him outside and reviewed the sacraments to him, placing particular stress on those sections that had to do with sin, punishment and hellfire. The Hallcomb boys, who had never received instruction in any of these subjects, stayed on the other side of the dusty street, grinning.

Thomas was outraged when the news came home to him. He nailed Kirby against the wall with his eyes. "Those are your mother's people," he said. "She would be mortified to know what you've done."

Kirby defiantly shook his head, denying any contrition. "They're not *my* people. I wouldn't claim them if she was *here*."

Thomas slapped him across the mouth, drawing blood. But he was too late. Much too late.

Afterward Thomas sat with me on the front steps, staring

sadly toward the family cemetery. "I gave him a bad name, Reed."

"No, Thomas," I said. "Kirby's a good name."

"He's wild, like the other Kirby was."

Wild yes, but there the similarity ended, I thought. The first Kirby had never hurt anyone except himself. The second Kirby hurt everybody around him. I didn't see that my saying so would do anybody any good, so I kept the feeling to myself.

Thomas made up his mind to put Kirby's excess energies to use. He sent him to Kansas with two thousand head of cattle and a tough-minded trail boss who had the disposition of an old wildcat with one foot in a trap. The boss brooked no foolishness. He made no distinction between the owner's son and the poorest Mexican cowhand in the crowd. When Kirby came home three months later he was lean, tanned and sober. He bore a small scar high on his cheek to remind him of the folly of challenging authority that was a head taller and forty pounds heavier.

For a while he applied himself to business and the school Thomas helped finance for youngsters in that part of the county. Any sign of backsliding could be stopped by reference to the possibility of another trip with that hard-driving trail boss.

Katy had been a little chubby as a small girl, but around twelve or thirteen she started growing up instead of out, taking on some of the look of her mother. She had those same wide brown eyes, a shy, sideways smile that often made me remember early trips I had made with Thomas to New Silesia. She must have made Thomas remember, too, for sometimes I caught him watching her with a sadness that put a chill on me. He had never completely buried Maria. Her ghost walked his house and lay with him in that big wooden bed.

From things Laura occasionally told me, and more she did not, I knew she did not share Thomas' bed. I knew they seldom talked to each other anymore, not about the things that really mattered. They spoke of the weather and the crops and the cattle, and of news in the San Antonio paper. That was enough to carry them through the meals. Afterward, each had a place in the house apart from the other, a retreat from the responsibility of conversation.

As Katy grew older, Thomas became increasingly uncomfortable around her. He appeared confused, uncertain, and he kept a relationship almost as formal as his with Laura. When Katy was fourteen Thomas sent her to San Antonio to boarding school, over Laura's protests. Laura went with her to see her settled and secure and was a month in coming home. That seemed to suit Thomas all right; in seeing after Katy she was performing the duties he had married her for.

Thomas seldom felt obliged to explain anything, but one night as we ate supper in the bunkhouse—Laura was still gone— he said to me, "Katy's by way of growing up. She'll be a woman before we know it. We have too many young men around this place who have no attachments and no responsibility. She needs to be gotten to a better climate."

I could not argue with him about that. Even at fourteen she had begun to distract some of the young hands from their work. I never did tell Thomas about the boy who kissed her and then tried to take her behind the barn. I would have thrashed him, but that seemed unnecessary after Katy had blacked both of his eyes and split his lip. I just fired him and told him to leave before Thomas somehow found out.

By the time she was sixteen, there was no telling what the situation might be.

Somehow, neither of us considered that there were boys in San Antonio too. Not that Katy was one to let her head be turned, but you don't solve a problem just by moving it out of your sight. When she came home to spend that first summer she seemed to get an awful lot of mail and spend much time with a pen in her hand, answering it.

She was near sixteen when she came home for the second

summer. Thomas was away on a land trip, for which I became thankful at the time. Laura had planned to take the buggy to San Antonio and fetch her, but all of a sudden and unannounced Katy showed up in front of the house in a buggy driven by a boy, or rather, a young man. He climbed down quickly and raised his hands to help her to the ground. Laura appeared on the porch, recognized Katy and hurried to the front gate with a smile I could see all the way from the corrals. The smile left her as she looked at the young man.

It was good to have the girl back on the place. I walked up from the corrals and hugged her like the uncle I was supposed to be. Katy pulled back and nodded toward the boy.

"Uncle Reed, I have somebody here I want you to meet."

The young man said, "We've met, Mr. Sawyer, a long time ago. I'm James Isom."

I've knocked down many a slaughter steer with the back side of an ax, and I felt as if somebody had just done that to me. An Isom here, on *this* place . . . It hadn't happened since the time Branch Isom had come out to try to buy some cattle from Thomas.

I shook the boy's hand and tried to remember how he had looked long ago when I had let his father have the cattle I had intended to buy. Now that I knew who he was, I could see he still had the same general features, the same big eyes that didn't look as if they ever had anything to hide. "It's good to see you again, son," I lied, thinking how fortunate it was that Thomas had gone somewhere.

Katy said, "James is going to school in San Antonio too, Uncle Reed. His mother and father went up to get him, and they offered to bring me home."

I could hardly believe what I heard. "You've been to Stonehill?" Her father had not set foot in that town since before she was born, except for a funeral. He had forbidden his children ever to go there. Kirby had violated that order for years, but I had never featured Katy doing it. I glanced at Laura but saw no

surprise. I suspected she had known the Isoms were sending
their boy to school in San Antonio. I also knew that if she had
ever told Thomas, he would have moved Katy to Galveston, or
maybe as far away as St. Louis or Kansas City.

Good manners meant I had to say something. All I could do
was ask him how his folks were. "Fine," he said. "Just fine." I
already knew that. Branch Isom had given up the cattle trade,
mainly because of competition from Thomas and me, and had
concentrated on business in Stonehill and on his freighting
trade, which still thrived. So long as the freight line stayed busy
he would prosper, and he didn't have to do anything illegal. So
would Stonehill, for it lived from the commerce that passed
through it going to and from the Gulf and the interior of Texas.

Katy said, "James, I hope you'll stay for supper."

Laura became very flustered. I pointed out how far it was
back to town. Even if he left now, James would have to make
part of the trip in the dark. I guess he understood the situation
better than Katy, because he agreed that he could not stay.

"I'll see you when school starts again," he told Katy.

She looked disappointed. "That's a long time."

"Not when you stay busy. I'll be helping my dad with the
business all summer. We'll see each other again before you
know it."

Katy watched him ride away on the old town road we didn't
use much. "He's a nice boy," she told Laura.

Laura put her arm around the girl's shoulder. "Come on into
the house. We have a lot to talk about before your father comes
home."

I was at the barn when Thomas rode in just at good dark,
looking weary. I could have unsaddled his horse for him, but
that was something a man did for himself. Worriedly he asked,
"Have you seen Kirby?"

"Yes, I sent him down to the south camp to help brand out
those calves."

"Good. I was afraid he might be off someplace with those Hallcomb boys, hunting for trouble."

I told him, "Katy came in a while ago."

Some of the weariness seemed to slide off of him. He smiled. "It sure is nice to have *one* child I don't have to worry about."

CHAPTER 8

The railroad rumors had risen periodically ever since the war, about as regularly as the big crops of grasshoppers that plagued us now and again. They always seemed reasonable enough. Somebody, someday, was bound to decide there was a profit to be made hauling goods from the coast by rail instead of by trail. I figured this fear must sometimes have awakened Branch Isom in the middle of a long night. Now the rumors started again, but this time there was a difference. A surveying party moved through the country. They made no secret of the fact that the newly-organized Gulf Coast and San Antonio Railroad planned to build along the general route of the old cart and wagon trails.

I expected Thomas to be pleased, but as usual he was looking farther ahead than I did. That was why I was still a little landowner and he was a big one. He said, "Sure, it'll be the end of Isom's mainline freight outfit, but they'll still need smaller lines to serve towns away from the rails. And a railroad will mean more prosperity for Stonehill than the freight trails did. Isom can throw the freight line away and still be richer than he ever was. He owns half of that wretched, damnable town." His face clouded over, and I was sorry I had brought up the subject.

There was a lot I didn't know about railroads. I guess I was like the fellow who buys crackers out of a barrel and figures they just grew that way. I had assumed somebody with a lot of money just came along and built the line. The people in Stonehill must have thought as I did. It came as a shock to them when the builder of the road arrived one day and asked for a sixty-thousand-dollar bonus to put his tracks through town. Their first inclination was to treat him to tar and feathers. As I heard it later, Branch Isom had a better grip on reality and advised that they study the proposition. Lamps burned far into the night at the big Isom house. Sixty thousand dollars was not a sum you snapped your fingers and called up easily, not in those days.

Our interest in the matter was only one of curiosity, because the route the surveyors had marked lay a couple of miles south of Thomas' land at the nearest point and a good dozen from mine. Thomas paid no attention to it. He predicted that the deal would blow apart anyway, and the railroad would never be built. Some sharp Yankee lawyer would get away with a lot of money and never be heard of again; it had happened before.

But one day while Thomas and I were at the corrals watching one of the Fernandez boys—men now, really—sack out a new bronc, a nice black carriage drew up to the big house. It had a Negro driver. A portly gentleman climbed down from the back seat and dusted himself. He looked up at the many front steps with dread.

Thomas called to him and saved him the climb. I followed along with Thomas. I had no real business there, but I gave in to curiosity, my biggest vice. We seldom saw such a rig at the ranch. It, and the gentleman who had arrived in it, reeked of money and importance.

I am sure the gray-bearded man sensed who Thomas was, but he went through the polite motions. "I have come to see Mr. Thomas Canfield?" He put it like a question.

Thomas introduced himself. The gentleman wasted no time with me; he could probably tell at a glance that I had about as much authority over major business decisions as one of Laura's white chickens scratching about the yard. "I am Jefferson P. Ashcroft, sir, vice-president of the GC and SA Railroad."

I had known right off that he had not come to sell hay and that he was no horse trader. Well, maybe he was, but of a higher order than those of my previous acquaintance.

"I have come on a matter of urgent business, Mr. Canfield," he said, fanning himself with his felt hat. Thomas led him to a bench Laura had placed beneath a big tree in the front yard. The man looked too tired to climb those front steps right now. He said, "You have perhaps heard of the impasse we have reached in our negotiations with the businessmen of Stonehill? We have asked what we feel is a reasonable bonus for placing a terminal in their city. They have not seen fit to meet our offer."

Thomas shrugged. "Stonehill's affairs are of no interest to me, Mr. Ashcroft. I have no interest in whether that town gets a railroad or not. For that matter, I do not care whether your railroad is ever built or not."

Ashcroft frowned. "I am given to understand that you are the largest landholder in this region. You ship thousands upon thousands of cattle each year."

"Drive, not ship. I have them driven."

"But sooner or later they are put upon a train. How much more beneficial would it be to you, sir, if you were able to ship them from right here on your property?"

"To where? Your railroad will go nowhere except to San Antonio and to the coast. My cattle go to Chicago and points east."

"Our railroad will someday connect with others."

"Someday! Someday I will be dead."

Ashcroft was a horse trader, all right. He recognized when he had a lame horse on his hands. "I shall lay my cards on the table, sir. As our route is surveyed it will cost us several miles of extra track to pass through Stonehill. We could cut our cost by building across your land."

There was not a trace of "give" in Thomas' eyes. "I am sure you could. And I suppose you would want me to pay you for the privilege."

Ashcroft seemed surprised at the thought. "No sir. We would buy your right-of-way at a fair price."

Thomas did not study the proposition long. "I buy land. I do not sell it. I would be happy to have you stay for supper, Mr. Ashcroft, but our business talk has come to an end."

Ashcroft was inclined to argue the point, but that look came into Thomas' eyes, the one that always turned away argument.

Laura came onto the porch as Ashcroft's carriage rounded the barn. "Mr. Canfield, wasn't your company staying for supper?"

Thomas shook his head. "No, Mrs. Canfield. His digestion seems poorly."

I have always sort of blamed the Hallcomb boys for what happened to Kirby, though I know the fault was not theirs alone. Kirby rode right into it himself. And I know you could blame Thomas, for not knowing how to give him a more right-eous upbringing. I even blame myself, remembering the times I should have put him over my knee instead of leaving that for Thomas when I knew he would not do it either, unless sorely provoked. A strong rod can sometimes help a tree grow straight and tall. Kirby bent with the wind.

It started, in a way, when the sheriff threw Speck Hallcomb in jail for beating up a San Antonio teamster he outweighed by thirty pounds. This put Speck in a mood for retaliation, a task for which he would need help. Kirby had not been running with the Hallcomb boys for a while; they had gotten along well enough without him. But Speck could not get out of jail, and Bo became tired of hunting up deviltry by himself, so he came out to the ranch and fetched Kirby when he knew Thomas was away from home. When Thomas returned, Kirby had been on a double-rectified drunk with Bo Hallcomb in Stonehill for three days. He was nineteen then, going on twenty, and tall for his age. Buying whisky was easy for him so long as he had the money. Thomas would not go to Stonehill himself to bring Kirby home; he sent the Fernandez brothers.

They brought Kirby home grimly, all three looking somewhat the worse for wear. The brothers would not talk about it, but I found out later that Kirby had fought them, saying some sorry things about their being nothing but a couple of dirty Mexicans who could not tell him what to do. Those were things they would not have heard from him had he been sober, for Marco and Juan had taught him most of what he knew about horse and cow work and most of the decent things he knew about life in general. But the things a man says when drunk are often those which have been on his mind when he was sober. The brothers did not have much to do with Kirby after that.

Thomas put Kirby to the dirtiest, meanest work he could find around the ranch. As usual, the reformation was shallow and short. Speck Hallcomb got out of jail in due time, nursing his grudges. He and Bo sneaked out to the south camp and took Kirby away with them. He did not need persuasion, just an opportunity.

The first any of us knew about it, the priest came hurrying down from the church in New Silesia, his buggy team lathered, his face furrowed with trouble. Thomas was gone, as usual. Laura sent for me. I knew when I looked at her and at the priest that something was badly wrong. Kirby and the Hallcomb boys had ridden into New Silesia roaring drunk and had shot up the place, running all the "potato-eaters" off of the street.

It was a merciful thing that both of the old Brozeks had gone to their reward and did not have to suffer through another humiliation at their grandson's hands, the priest lamented.

Laura cried softly. She looked older than she really was; part of it was Thomas, but a lot of it, I knew, was Kirby. "Reed, maybe you can talk to him. Please, bring him home," she said.

It had been a long time since Kirby had talked much to me, and longer since he had listened to me. I had to call on all the persuasive powers I had to convince Marco and Juan that they should go with me. They had not forgotten the last time, and probably they never would. I managed to convey to them my concern that Kirby might require stronger persuasion than I was physically able to give.

We arrived in New Silesia too late. Kirby and the Hallcombs had moved on to richer game, to Stonehill, where Speck still had a score he wanted to mark off. New Silesia normally was a quiet little place where you still heard more Polish spoken on the streets than English. The only local law was a little constable whose most strenuous normal duty was chasing schoolboys home at dark to study their books. Kirby and the Hallcombs had buffaloed him the first ten minutes they were in town; he had not come back outside again until they left.

He spent a minute or two telling me what he would do if they ever came back, then said darkly, "Stonehill is not New Silesia. They will kill somebody there, or be killed."

I did not want to take him all that seriously, but I got a cold feeling in my stomach. I glanced at Marco and Juan. Their eyes told me they had it too. We set our horses into a long trot for Stonehill. For the animals' sake I tried to hold the pace to that, but in a while I was loping, and the brothers were close beside me.

The New Silesia–Stonehill road led by the Goodson Hallcomb farm. As we passed it, Speck and Bo Hallcomb came riding out. I hailed them. They glanced at us but kept riding. I had to spur a tired horse to catch up to them. I rode past and turned around to face them before they would stop. They were cold sober, both of them, and scared.

"Where's Kirby?" I demanded. Neither would look at me. I asked them again. The Fernandez brothers pushed in behind them, adding to the pressure.

Speck still would not look at me, but he said, "It was Kirby done it, not us. We didn't figure on anything going that far."

I grabbed the front of his shirt and shook him. "Did what?"

"He shot and killed the sheriff. We tried to stop him, but he went and done it anyway. Now you got to let us go, Mr. Sawyer. Them people'll be coming after us."

"What people?"

"The whole town, I expect. We turned and lit out when we seen the sheriff go down. Seemed like the whole town was shooting at Kirby, and at us too."

"You went off and left him there by himself?"

"Them was awful mad people."

I put spurs to my horse, cursing and praying at the same time. I could hear the Fernandez brothers pushing to stay close behind me. We were still in a lope as we hit the edge of town. I reined up to look for a minute. The chill came back, for the place was quiet, much too quiet. Not a wagon was rolling. I saw a few horsemen milling around, and people standing in clusters. Whatever had happened was over and done. I could not bring myself to look at the brothers, but I knew they must share the cold dread that came over me like a winter fog. We walked our hard-breathing horses down the street. The people turned to stare, and I felt anger and hostility rising against us. Everybody knew who we were.

A familiar figure walked out into the street and stood waiting. Branch Isom had put on weight the last few years. He was not exactly portly, but prosperity had made him comfortable and soft, a far cry from the muscular, driving man I remembered from my first acquaintance with him in old Indianola town. I noted that he was not armed, though nearly everyone else on the street was.

We stopped our horses a few feet from him. He seemed to be looking beyond us. "Is Thomas Canfield on his way?" he asked.

I sensed right off that the town was braced for invasion. They took us for the vanguard. I hoped they could see we were not carrying guns. "We haven't seen him," I said. "Where's Kirby?"

Isom did not answer me directly. "You know what he did?

He killed the sheriff. Wounded a couple of other people, too."

"We just heard about the sheriff from the Hallcomb boys. We didn't know about anybody else. Where's Kirby?" I was afraid I knew better, but I added, "You have him in jail?"

Isom shook his head and turned, beckoning. The people had moved out into the street as if to block us, but they stepped back and made room as Isom led us fifty yards to the open livery barn. Beneath a brush arbor, on a pile of hay, lay an old gray blanket. I knew what was under it and did not want to look as Isom pulled it back, but I forced myself.

Kirby must have been shot twenty times.

Isom said, "I wouldn't have had it happen for the world. But the way things were, people didn't have a choice. He had to be stopped."

I supposed he was right, but the grief and the anger and the cold nausea all came up on me just the same. They did not have to shoot him to pieces.

"Who-all did it, Branch?" I asked.

He let the blanket down gently. "All I can tell you is that I was not among them. Don't ask me to tell you more."

"Thomas will ask you."

"I hoped you would head him off, Sawyer. If he comes in here boiling for trouble, he'll find it. This town is in a black mood. I'll have a wagon fetched around so you can take Kirby home. Try and keep Thomas away from here. Please!"

It was hard to realize this was the same Branch Isom I had known so long ago. There had been a time he would have stood in the middle of the street and dared Thomas to come. Now he was begging me for peace.

"I have worked hard to get this town a respectable name, to live down what it used to be," he continued. "Now we have a railroad coming in. We don't want any more trouble here."

I said, "Bring the wagon."

The hostility of the people was silent but as real as a pit of rattlesnakes. Juan and Marco and I lifted Kirby into the wagon and covered him with the blanket. Nobody offered to help. Juan climbed onto the wagon seat. Isom handed him the lines and looked back at me. "For God's sake, Sawyer, keep Thomas away from here!"

A shout lifted from the far end of the street. My heart came to my throat as I saw a group of riders coming, fanned out in a wedge. Townspeople pulled back to the porches and wooden sidewalks, making room.

"It's too late," I said. "He's here."

Thomas' face was gray as he rode up the street. He stopped before the wagon, his jaw set like a block of stone. He stared at the covered form. The voice did not sound like his.

"Pull back the blanket."

Juan started to obey. I reined my horse in close and caught the corner of the blanket. "No, Thomas. You don't want to, not here."

Thomas' eyes cut me like a knife. He bumped his horse's shoulder against mine and pushed me aside. He lifted the blanket for himself. His cheekbones seemed to bulge. His eyes glassed over. When he turned, he was in a wild rage. He fixed his gaze on Branch Isom.

"Who did it?"

Branch Isom had lost color, but he did not back away. "Your boy killed the sheriff, Thomas. He was shooting up the town."

"I want to know who-all did this to him!"

"Nobody wanted this. I know how you feel, Thomas; I've got a boy of my own. If there'd been any other way . . ."

"Damn you, Isom! I don't want to take on this whole town, but I'll do it if I don't see the men who did this to my boy. You call them out here!"

Thomas' hand was on the butt of his pistol. My throat went dry as I looked at the cowboys he had brought with him . . . *gringos*, Mexicans . . . he had never made much distinction so long as they did their work. They were scared, most of them, looking into the guns of half that town. But they also appeared determined. If Thomas said the word, war would explode then and there. Seeing those wild and ungiving eyes, I was sure Thomas was about to give that word. We were badly outnumbered, but not one man of Thomas' crew pulled back or showed any sign of the feather. No less was tolerated of a man in those days; he was expected to be loyal to the brand he worked for and die for it, if circumstances carried him to that. Marco and Juan and I were unarmed, but I knew we would be shot down with the rest.

I said, "Thomas, Kirby was in the wrong."

Thomas did not respond.

Cold sweat glistened on Branch Isom's round, reddish face. "For the love of God, Thomas, look around you. There's two men dead already. You pull that gun and there may be twenty."

"You'll be the first one."

Isom's shoulders slumped. I thought he had given up. Then he said something I would never have expected. "Shoot me, then, if it'll satisfy you. Shoot me and let my town alone."

Thomas seethed. "I should have shot you twenty years ago. I had the chance, once. I've always been sorry I didn't do it."

Fear was plain in Isom's eyes, but he did not back away.

Thomas said, "You're not armed."

"I haven't carried a gun in years."

"Get one."

Isom brought himself to look in Thomas' terrible eyes. "No. You'll have to shoot me as I am."

Thomas drew the pistol halfway out of the holster, and thirty men brought up their guns. Isom stood watching him, his face frozen. He did not plead. He did not move his feet.

Thomas seemed oblivious to the guns raised against him. He never took his eyes from Isom's face. "One last time, Isom, tell me who killed him."

Isom said nothing. He held his eyes to Thomas', and after a long moment it was Thomas who looked away.

"Whoever you are," he shouted to the town, "whoever shot my boy, come out here and face me!"

Nobody answered. Nobody came.

Thomas let the pistol slip back into the holster. His gaze ran the length of the street, touching on every man. His voice rose so that everybody on the street could hear. "Then you *all* killed him. This whole town killed him, the way it's killed almost everybody I ever cared about in my life. This town killed my father. It killed my brother, and my mother, and my wife. Now it's killed my son!"

He paused. I could not hear a sound except the nervous movement of horses, the squeak of saddle leather.

Thomas stood in his stirrups and raised his fist over his head. In a voice that must have carried out onto the prairie he shouted, "This town has killed the last of mine. I swear by Almighty God, I am going to kill this town!"

He reined his horse around and moved back down the street. The crowd melted aside as the Red Sea must have parted for Moses. The cowboys, much relieved, turned their horses and followed him. I felt weak enough to fall out of my saddle. I nodded at Juan, still on the wagon. "Let's go."

I tried not to look at the townspeople, though I had to give one more glance to Branch Isom. He looked drained and limp and incredibly sad. But he never moved.

We buried Kirby in the family plot on the slope, beside the uncle whose unlucky name he bore. Staring at the weathered stone with the first Kirby's name on it, I thought of the many ways in which the two young men had been alike, impetuous, even wild. But the first Kirby had sought nothing more than fun; there had never been anything little about him, or mean.

Mostly I watched Thomas during the ceremony. Laura held his arm at first, trying to give him comfort. But Thomas seemed to draw away, shutting her out. He stood alone. Laura put her arms around Katy, and the two women wept quietly together.

As the minister finished his final prayer, the little crowd dutifully came by in an informal line and expressed their condolences, the custom of the country, a burden the bereaved were expected to endure stoically. Thomas received them with a stony face and a mechanical manner. The last two men to come up were strangers, each wearing a circular badge with a star in its center. One of them asked, "Could we talk with you a minute, Mr. Canfield? Somewhere in private?"

Thomas blinked, taken by surprise. His stony look returned. "This is private enough."

The Rangers were ill at ease. The spokesman said, "We've been sent from San Antonio to keep the peace."

"It's a little late, don't you think?"

"We were sent to be sure nothing more happens. Our orders are to do anything necessary to see that it doesn't. Anything."

Thomas' eyes narrowed. His gaze dropped to the pistols both men wore prominently on their hips. "If I were going to shoot up Stonehill, I would have done it yesterday."

"You made a threat about killing the town."

"I intend to," he said coldly. "And there won't be one thing you or anybody can do about it."

He turned from the Rangers as if they were not there. He drew me away from the crowd and asked, "Do you have any idea where that railroad man is, that Ashcroft?"

I thought he might be in Stonehill, but there was no way to know except by going and seeing for myself. I did not want to go to Stonehill.

Thomas said, "Please, Reed, go for *me*. Go for Kirby. Find him if you have to ride all the way to San Antonio. Fetch him here."

I began to sense some of what was in his mind. It made me feel sad. "Thomas, you don't really want to do this."

He looked me in the eyes, and I could not hold against his stare. "If you don't go, I will," he said.

It was ticklish, riding into Stonehill. My skin prickled at the sight of the town. Its streets seemed deserted. Most of the people were at the cemetery, showing the sheriff's family their support at the funeral. The Canfield ranch had few friends left in that place, but I sought out one of those few who might know something of the railroad man. He told me Ashcroft had departed Stonehill in anger the day before the shooting, bound for San Antonio.

I spent the night on the road, stopping for a few hours' sleep on the ground. I found Ashcroft in the Menger Hotel bar, where he had been paying homage to the state of Kentucky for most of three days. He was in little mood to talk to anyone from Stonehill or its environs. "Robbers and thieves, all of them," he grumbled, "hoping to enrich themselves at the expense of the railroad."

I explained that I had nothing to do with Stonehill but represented Thomas Canfield instead. His resentment survived intact.

"I suppose Mr. Canfield has decided to sell us a right-of-way and enrich himself at our expense also."

He had no intention of coming with me. I thought of force but rejected that because I knew San Antonio had a high ratio of policemen to citizens and would not tolerate that kind of behavior. I sat with him in the bar and plied him with Bourbon until he went to sleep in his chair. Had he died then and there, the undertaker would have had nothing to do but place him in a box. I rented a carriage from a wagonyard, loaded him into it and started for the ranch. We had put many miles behind us before he rallied enough to realize he was on the road. He cursed me for twelve kinds of blackguard and threatened me with a lifetime in Huntsville penitentiary, but he had no wish to walk back to San Antonio. It was far past midnight when we reached the ranch, and he was cold sober.

Thomas dressed and met Ashcroft in the front parlor. He got right to the point.

"Mr. Ashcroft, are you still interested in a right-of-way across my ranch?"

Ashcroft blustered. "Kidnapping me and dragging me out here is a poor way of doing business. If you think we are going to pay you some exorbitant price . . ."

Thomas did not let him finish. He leaned forward, into the man's face. His eyes had the look of a hawk at the kill. "I'll *give* you the land!"

He had Ashcroft's total attention, and mine. "Give it?"

"With conditions. I want you to route your rails as far from Stonehill as you can."

Ashcroft blinked a few times. "We need Stonehill."

"No you don't. If you need a town, build one. I'll give you the land for that too."

Ashcroft was momentarily shocked beyond speech. He stared at me as if he did not quite believe, as if he feared he might still be drunk and dreaming all this.

"I don't understand."

"You don't have to understand. All you have to do is agree."

Ashcroft mumbled, benumbed. "I am not certain I can speak for the board of directors . . ."

"To hell with the directors. Just say *yes.*"

Ashcroft was still looking for a catch but could not see one. "Well, yes," he sputtered. "Of course, yes."

Not until that moment had I realized the full depth of Thomas' hatred, the sacrifice he was willing to make for revenge. I could not remember that he had ever sold a square foot of land; once he had gotten hold of it, he had held it fiercely. Now he was giving it away.

I stared at the fire in Thomas' eyes, and at the bewilderment in Ashcroft's.

I said, "There's a passage in the Bible, Thomas. Vengeance is mine, saith the Lord."

He shook his head.

"No. This time, it's *mine.*"

CHAPTER 9

The surveyors had been working their way across the ranch for several days before the people of Stonehill got their first inkling. Quickly Branch Isom consulted other community leaders and offered the railroad the bonus Ashcroft had originally asked. When he refused it, they raised thirty thousand more. It was too late. The railroad had signed the contracts with Thomas and saved itself thousands of dollars in right-of-way investment. This was at Thomas' expense, of course, but if he ever gave the cost a moment's notice he betrayed no sign.

Stonehill should have had a long, slow period of grace before its decline; railroads are not built overnight. But dry rot set in with the realization that the wheels were in motion and that there would be no reversal of plans for going around. Though freight lines still passed through the town, and would until the trains were running—and though wagon service would still be needed to the border and to towns that lay south and north of the railroad—the heart quickly was gone from Stonehill. One by one, businesses began to be boarded up or moved away.

Branch Isom tried desperately to hold the place together. He argued that branch lines serving the railroad would still bring commerce to Stonehill streets, that many ranchers and farmers would still choose Stonehill as their place to trade. He pointed out that it was the county seat and still had the courthouse. He even made rash guarantees of financial support in a desperate effort to keep his town alive.

The railroad platted a new town on its right-of-way. A few

buildings were up even before the rails reached it, an evidence
of more faith than I could have mustered. There was some
question about a proper name. The railroad people first
suggested it be called Canfield, but Thomas rejected that notion
as self-advertisement. He wanted to name it Brozekville, for
Maria's family. The railroad people thought that sounded too
foreign. When Washington approved the post office, the chosen
name turned out to be Ashcroft City. Thomas fumed over that
a few days, but the cause was lost. One area always foreign to
him was politics.

He still carried weight with the railroad, however, and the
power of veto over who could buy property in Ashcroft City.
At first he would allow no one from Stonehill to own property
in his town. But soon he realized that the way to drain Stonehill
and leave Branch Isom presiding over a dead town was to give
people there another place to go. Once he made up his mind to
that, and swallowed the fact that he would have to tolerate at
least some of the Stonehill citizens in the new town, he saw to it
that the lots in Ashcroft City were sold cheaply enough for anybody to buy one. He screened the buyers, turning away some of
Stonehill's more notorious denizens. He put it down as an
ironclad rule that no property would be sold to Branch Isom or
any of his kin.

Once the tracks were laid through town and stretched west-
ward toward San Antonio, the exodus from Stonehill turned
into a stampede. Thomas financed several of his cowboys who
had higher ambitions. They invested in teams and heavy
timber-moving equipment, which they converted to the moving
of frame buildings. It was no great engineering feat to jack up a
small structure, put runners under it and move it the ten or
twelve miles from Stonehill to Ashcroft City.

Thomas was getting what he wanted, but he never smiled. I
sensed it was not enough.

One day while we were working cattle on the south part of
the ranch, not far from Stonehill, one of the chuck-wagon

mules became entangled in the traces, and the wagon fetched up in a gully with a broken wheel. I took the wheel to Stonehill to have a wheelwright fix it. The sight of the place hit me like a fist between the eyes. It looked as if half the houses were gone, jacked up and hauled away, leaving nothing but the cedar-post foundations on which they had stood standing like broken ribs of a wolf-eaten carcass. Most of the businesses still operating belonged to Branch Isom; the other storekeepers and artisans for the most part had left, bound for Ashcroft City or San Antonio or points west. Traffic was so slow that chickens scratched in the middle of the street.

The only smithy and wheelwright still operating worked in a shop which serviced the Isom freight wagons. He assured me he could get to my wheel right away; he had nothing else to do.

I walked down the street past empty stores, past empty lots where stores had stood. I stepped into a bar and had a drink. The bartender seemed glad to see me, though he knew full well who I was and who I represented. He and I were the only people in the place.

The drink seemed sour, and I did not tarry long. I walked on down to Isom's big mercantile store, where a lone farm wagon stood out front. I was tempted to go in but didn't know what, if anything, I could say to Branch Isom. Suddenly he was standing in the door, staring at me in surprise. I could not pretend I had not seen him. I said howdy, not knowing anything that seemed appropriate.

"You'd just as well come on in, Reed Sawyer," he said. "No use standing out in the sun."

I walked into the store and stood awkwardly, making small talk about the weather and how we needed a rain. I don't think Isom paid much attention to what I said, any more than I paid to his make-talk efforts. Finally I blurted out what was really on my mind. "Goddammit, Branch, I'm sorry."

Isom went silent awhile, then said, "I guess it would've been better if Thomas and I had shot it out with each other a long time ago. Whichever way it went, it would've saved a lot of people a lot of grief."

"Why don't you just leave here, Branch, and start over someplace else? You could do good in San Antonio."

"This is my town. Everything I own is tied up here. I have no choice but to ride it to the end of the line."

I was about to say it might be a short ride, but I kept that observation to myself. I said, "It's not much of a future for your boy."

"James will be all right. He has a good position in a bank in San Antonio. He's a smart boy, even if he *is* mine. You watch, he'll be a wealthy man someday. They'll put up a statue of him in a San Antonio park."

I caught that pride in his eyes, the kind of pride Thomas had never been able to have in Kirby. Strange, I thought, how the seed can sometimes produce a tree so much different than the one it came from.

I told Isom I had not seen his son in a long time. He said, "He's home for a visit." I heard a jingle of trace chains through the open back door. Isom turned an ear in that direction. "I'll bet that's him now."

In a moment a pair of shadows fell through the open door. A girl entered, followed by a slender young man. My mouth dropped open.

"Katy!"

Katy Canfield was so startled that she dropped her purse. James Isom stooped to pick it up and place it back in her hands. She stared at me with big, pretty brown eyes, disconcerted. "Uncle Reed, what're you doing here?"

"I'm a grown man; I can go where I want to. But you're not a grown woman yet, not quite. Your daddy have any idea where you are?"

She took a minute to answer. "Mother knows."

Somehow that did not surprise me. Kirby's raising, such as it was, had been mostly Thomas' doing. But the raising of Katy had been left mostly to Laura. Katy and Laura had always drawn together, two women combining their strength against a man's world of land and cattle and commerce.

Katy had much of the look of the mother she barely remembered. But I could not recall that I had ever seen so much trouble in Maria's eyes.

I said, "This is the last place in the world your daddy would want to see you."

"He's wrong; you know that."

"But he *is* your daddy."

James Isom touched Katy's arm, and she leaned to him for support. I had known they both went to school in San Antonio, and I remembered the time James had brought her home. But *this* . . . The idea had never entered my mind.

There was no pretending I had not seen. "How serious is it between you two?"

James said evenly, "It's serious, Mr. Sawyer."

I could see Katy's answer in her eyes. She said, "Uncle Reed, do you have to tell him?"

I studied the pair, clinging together. James was a clean-looking young man, his face appearing honest and without guile. He said, "I love her, Mr. Sawyer."

Branch Isom told me, "It's been none of my doing. I've tried to talk them out of it. But if you've ever been in love, Reed, I guess you know how little good it does to talk."

My stomach drew into a knot. I could remember.

Katy touched my arm. "Uncle Reed, if you think he has to know, let me be the one to tell him. Please, give me a little time. I'll have to find a way of my own."

I said, "You kids know he'll find out sooner or later . . . someday, some way. But it won't come from me."

They drew against one another, and Katy thanked me.

Though much of Stonehill's population wound up in Ashcroft City, it would be a mistake to think of that place simply as Stonehill transplanted. The building of the railroad, a round-house and service facilities brought in a lot of new people, enough to give Ashcroft City a different political complexion. Even while Stonehill was still the county seat, Ashcroft City began electing most of the county officers. And it was not meant that Stonehill keep the county courthouse forever. In the Ashcroft City plat was a block in the center of town, reserved for a new county courthouse. When Ashcroft City had the political power firmly in its grip, an election was called to decide whether to move the county seat. Branch Isom and his hangers-on tried hard, electioneering diligently among the country folk. But the issue was lost long before election day. Ashcroft City carried five to three. A bond issue was passed for a new stone courthouse, bigger and better than the old frame structure in Stonehill. In due course the building was completed. The only task remaining was the transfer of the county records.

This process, though it had the full backing of law, had caused bloodshed in several old Texas counties as they outgrew their original county seats and attempted a move. The ballot was one thing; possession was another.

The sheriff and one of his deputies, Ashcroft City men both, were met at the courthouse one day by a group of armed Stone-hill men who blocked their entrance and served notice they did not intend to allow movement of the county records. They denied the lawmen access to their own office. The sheriff went directly to Thomas, who called in all his cowboys. I could see a grim satisfaction in Thomas' eyes as he stood on the steps of his house with the sheriff, the rest of us spread out on the ground. The sheriff swore all of us in as deputies. We rode together to Ashcroft City, where he swore in enough townsmen to give him a posse of sixty or seventy.

It was my bad luck to have been at the headquarters at all that day. I had begun trying to take care of my own business, my own cattle, and had even built a small frame house on my place. Personally I didn't much give a damn which town had the courthouse. I tried to tell Thomas so, but as always when he had his mind set on something he did not listen. He just nodded, taking it for granted that I was agreeing with him on everything.

I should simply have ridden away, but Thomas still had that power to pull people to him, and I was not immune from it.

We trooped down the wagon road to Stonehill like a ragged cavalry unit, guns bristling. A lot of the younger men were bragging about what they would do if it came to a fight, hoping it would. Pleasure showed in Thomas' face, too, which fed the uneasiness growing in me. Having been in that other war, I had already enjoyed about all this type of conflict that I ever wanted.

Behind us rumbled half a dozen empty freight wagons, enough to haul not only the county records but most of the courthouse furniture. Thomas and I rode up front, with the sheriff. Thomas said, "This is about what I expected from Branch Isom. If he puts up a fight, I want everybody to remember: he's mine."

I should have been angry at Stonehill for its resistance to the law, but I found myself angering at Thomas instead. I said, "The Texas Rangers could handle this, and nobody would get hurt."

Thomas declared solemnly, "We don't need the Rangers, or anybody else from outside. This is our business."

I let my exasperation rise into my voice. "You'll never rest easy till you've killed him!"

Thomas flashed me a look of surprise, which turned into doubt. His anger arose to meet mine. He said, "Reed, something has been gnawing at you lately. You've been partners with me for a long time, but if you're wanting to leave . . ."

I had not fully realized it, but suddenly I knew that I did. It was time to make a full break, as I had intended to years earlier when he married Laura.

I said, "I know Branch Isom a lot better than you do. At

least let me go talk to him first. Maybe there won't be a need for anybody to get hurt."

His anger built. "You *don't* know Branch Isom. You never did."

"You just know him as he used to be. People change. He doesn't want to be your enemy; he hasn't wanted to in a long time. He's just old, and he's tired. Like us."

"I'm not tired." Thomas gave me a long, hard study. "If that's the way you feel, maybe you'd better ride on ahead and stand up with him."

"If the time comes that I feel like I should, I will."

I half expected him to explode, but instead he cooled. The look in his eyes was of hurt, of puzzlement.

After a time he said, "You don't mean that, Reed. We've been together too long."

"Like I said, people change. *You've* changed, and most of it hasn't been any improvement."

I watched him as we moved into Stonehill. I do not think he had seen the place since the day Kirby was killed. I do not believe he was fully prepared for the shell that Stonehill had become. It was as if a tornado had skipped through and had taken half the buildings away, damaging many of the rest.

"Good God!" he exclaimed.

I told him, "You *said* you'd kill this town. You've done it."

"I haven't killed *all* of it. *He's* still here."

We rode straight for the old courthouse. Its two stories had been built originally of green lumber so that the siding was beginning to twist and curl in places. The long comb along the roof had a gentle sag in the middle, like an old horse needing retirement to green pasture. But lined in front of it were fifteen or twenty men with pistols, rifles and shotguns in their hands. They were a pitiful remnant compared to the force Stonehill might once have offered; we had them badly outnumbered.

The sheriff made a wide motion with his hand, signaling his posse to spread out. He rode in front, his hands high against his

chest and far from his weapons, reins in the left hand, a sheaf
of papers in the right. He tried to pick out the leader of the
Stonehill defense. Branch Isom was not among them.

I glanced at Thomas. His eyes betrayed disappointment.
Then they lifted. I swung around to see what he had seen.
Branch Isom was coming out onto the porch of his big house
on the hill.

The sheriff was saying, "Gentlemen, you all know who I am.
You know the authority I represent. I have here the official
canvass of the vote, making Ashcroft City the county seat. I
also have here an order from the district court that all county
records be duly removed to Ashcroft City. I ask that you step
aside and let the law peacefully take its course."

Half the men talked at once, or tried to. This group had no
leader. That could be good, or it could be bad. A leaderless
group of angry men was unpredictable.

The sheriff, still in his saddle, made a move toward the
courthouse. Three men jumped forward and grabbed the reins
and bit. He shouted, "In the name of the law . . ."

Thomas drew his pistol. Branch Isom was running down the
hill toward us, waving his hands. The commotion around the
sheriff was so loud I could not hear what Isom was shouting. I
put my hand firmly over Thomas', pressing down against his
pistol.

"Wait," I said. He struggled angrily to free his hand, but I
held tight.

Isom's face was flushed. He breathed heavily from the exer-
tion of the run. Age and soft living had sapped the strength and
endurance of his youth. "Sheriff," he said urgently, "please
hold off a minute. Let me talk to these men."

Through gritted teeth Thomas said, "We don't care to listen
to you, Isom."

The sheriff turned in a fury that surprised me. "Mr.
Canfield," he said, "*I* am in charge here."

Thomas said, "The hell you are." He tried again to raise the pistol, but I pressed it hard against the horn of his saddle. He cursed me.

Isom turned his back on us and addressed the men who had chosen to defend Stonehill.

"Friends, I asked you before. I *plead* with you now. The law is with them. They have you outnumbered. Even if you beat them today they'll be back tomorrow with more. They'll bring the Rangers, or even the army. Give it up now, and let's not have anybody die. Too many have died already for lost causes."

Most of them seemed to be listening to him. Perhaps they were looking for an excuse to back away from a fight they could readily see they would lose. But it seemed to me they were listening to him with respect, the way men in this town once listened to old Linden Hines.

It came to me with a sudden jolt that Branch Isom, even in his wild younger days, had respected Linden Hines. He had respected him so much that—perhaps unconsciously—he had taken the old man's place.

Isom saw the men's hesitation, their doubt. He pounced on it.

"Tobe Haney, you have two good kids. You want to take a chance on dying now, when they need you the most? Bill, who's going to take care of your old mother? This courthouse means very little to her, but you mean all there is."

Thomas stared at Isom in disbelief and deep disappointment. He had wanted Isom to be the ringleader here, not the peacemaker. I let go of the pistol. Thomas burned me with a look of resentment.

He had watched Branch Isom so intently that he had not noticed James following his father down from the big house. Now James stood beside Branch, saying nothing but lending his silent support. Thomas studied him. I saw the sudden stiffness when recognition came. Thomas' jaw hardened.

He knew, I realized. Somehow, he knew.

The fuse still sputtered, but Branch Isom had pulled it from the powder. The Stonehill men began to draw aside, muttering grudgingly but without violence. The sheriff climbed the short steps and threw open the courthouse doors. He signaled for the wagons to be brought up. He was suddenly in a hurry, wanting to be done with this before someone fired the fuse again. The Ashcroft City men marched into the courthouse without fanfare, without cheering. A few were probably disappointed about the avoidance of a fight, but I think the majority were relieved whether they would ever admit it or not; the sight of the other side with guns in their hands had taken a lot of the romance out of the showdown.

Branch Isom moved closer to Thomas. "All right, you've won." Bitterness edged his voice, but resignation was there, too. "What little is left of my town, you'll be hauling away in those wagons."

Thomas seemed not to hear. His eyes were on young Isom. They were the hawk eyes I dreaded so much. He said, "You'd be Branch Isom, Jr., wouldn't you?"

"James Isom," the young man quietly corrected him.

"Well, Branch Isom, Jr., my quarrel with your father is an old one. My quarrel with you is new. You know what I'm talking about?"

James's eyes did not waver. "I guess I do."

"I intend it to stop, now! I'll send her to Europe, if I have to. And I'll send you to hell!"

Thomas cut his gaze back to Branch. "I had a son. You remember how I lost him. If you don't want to lose yours, you'd better talk to him!"

He pulled hard on the reins, turning his horse half around. He stopped and looked at me. "You have something to say?"

I did. "You'd have killed half the men here, just to settle your own private feud."

"Yes," he said flatly, "I would have. You coming?"

My stomach was cold. I said, "No."

"Stay here, then. Stay with Branch Isom."

I found myself giving voice to a notion that had been rising in me. "*He's* not Branch Isom, not anymore. *You* are!"

What I said never reached him, not to the point that he understood. He shrugged. "Suit yourself," he said, and left there in a long trot, his cowboys following him. I watched them until they were on the trail, then I turned and headed for the saloon.

I never had much luck solving my problems in a whisky glass. When the glass was empty the problems were still there, as big as ever. I nursed a couple of slow drinks, however, trying to decide what to do next. I did not lack for a place to go. My ranch was nowhere nearly so large as Thomas', but it was mine. I had gone there often to see after my cattle, sometimes staying several days. But always I had gone "home" afterward. "Home" had always been Thomas' place.

I knew it never would be again.

I heard horses on the street occasionally but paid little attention, mulling over my own problems. I became aware of a man standing in the open doorway, blocking much of the light. "Reed?" he called. "Reed Sawyer?"

I was startled to see Branch Isom there, a rifle in his hand. My heart bumped with the thought that the rifle was for me, because I had ridden into town with Thomas' invading army.

Urgently Isom said, "Reed Sawyer, I need your help."

The whisky had gone to my head a little. Whisky always had a tendency to make me sullen, one reason I drank so little of it. At that moment I was mad at everybody. "The hell you say."

"Reed," he said, "you've got little cause to look on me as a friend, but at least I hope you don't see me as your enemy."

The whisky's glow began to fade. "What's your trouble?"

He stepped closer. For the first time I saw a cut at the corner of his mouth, a bruise starting to purple. "It's James. That fool boy has gone to the Canfield ranch to get that girl. I tried to stop him."

I was cold sober. "Thomas'll kill him!"

"Not if I can get there first. You have any influence over Thomas?"

I shook my head. "*Nobody* has any influence over Thomas."

"I wish you'd come along and try. I don't want to kill him, but I'll do it to keep that crazy bastard from killing my boy."

In my haste to get up from the table I turned over the bottle. It fell to the floor and went rolling, spilling whisky. In a few long strides I was out of the place and into the saddle, riding out of town in a hard lope. I had to spur to keep Isom from pulling far out in front of me.

At times we could glimpse James at some distance ahead. He had seen us and knew we would try to stop him, so he held his lead. When we speeded up, he speeded up. We could not run the horses long at a time, or they would not endure to take us to the ranch headquarters. We would lope awhile, then slow to a trot to let them catch their wind. I told Isom there was a chance Thomas would not be at home. But the tracks along the trail told me Thomas and the cowboys had come this way ahead of us.

James arrived at the Canfield house a few minutes before we did. That was more than time enough. As we rode through the open gate of the outer corral, I saw someone fighting on the broad porch.

Isom's face twisted in fear. He shouted vainly against the wind. "Wait! Wait!"

Someone fell backward off of the high steps. It had to be James, for Thomas stood on the porch, pistol in his hand. Katy struggled with him. As we spurred up I could hear her screaming, pleading with him. Laura was there too, trying to hold Thomas' arm. He gave her a rough push. Laura stumbled and fell backward over a chair. Thomas pulled free of his daughter and shoved her violently. She fell over Laura. Thomas started down the steps toward James, the pistol pointed.

"Canfield!" Branch Isom shouted. He jumped from his horse

and sprinted defensively toward his son. James was on one knee. I knew at a glance that he was not armed. He had not come here to kill; he had probably realized that if he brought a gun he might be forced to use it.

Thomas swung the pistol toward Branch Isom. I was off my horse and running toward him. "Thomas, don't!"

Thomas fired. Branch Isom stumbled, his hat spinning from his head. He pitched to the ground. The rifle clattered from his hands. He had not had time to pull the trigger.

Thomas' face was a roaring fire. The pistol had leaped in recoil, and he lowered it to fire again. I managed to grab his arm.

"For God's sake, Thomas, come to your senses!"

I had never realized how powerful he was, especially with the fury pounding hot. He flung me backward, off balance. I saw the pistol swinging at me and tried vainly to throw myself out of its path. If my hat had not cushioned it, the heavy gun barrel would probably have broken my skull. I felt my face slam against the ground, and dirt was in my eyes. I raised up, trying to clear my throbbing head.

Now instead of Branch trying to protect his son, James rushed to his father.

"No, Mr. Canfield! Please don't shoot him again!"

Red and white flashes went off like fireworks before my eyes, and my head pounded. In spite of that, I saw Katy run down the steps and across the yard. She picked up the fallen rifle as her father raised the muzzle of his pistol against James.

Cold dread crawled up my back. Katy was about to kill her father. I said something akin to prayer, rolled onto my side and drew my six-shooter. As Thomas half turned, steadying his pistol, I squeezed the trigger. The recoil wrenched it from my weak hand. Through the gray smoke I saw Thomas stagger, drop to his knees, then sink awkwardly onto one shoulder.

Katy stared at him in horror, the rifle unfired but pointed at him.

Laura cried out and ran down the steps, taking them two at a time. Katy lowered the rifle, her eyes wide in shock. I believe that for a moment she thought she had shot her father.

Legs shaky, James hurried to her and took her in his arms. The rifle slipped into the dust.

Laura dropped to her knees and threw her arms around Thomas, pulling him against her. "Thomas! Thomas!"

He groaned, so I knew he was not dead. I glanced at Branch Isom. He was trying to push himself to a sitting position. Blood ran down the side of his face from the crease Thomas' bullet had given him. James pulled away from Katy and went to his father's side, crying out in relief that Branch was not dead.

Katy stood alone, staring in disbelief at her fallen father.

Laura hugged Thomas and begged him not to die. I managed to get my feet under me and stagger to Thomas' side. I slumped to my knees and tore his shirt open. I had put a bullet into his shoulder.

"Branch Isom," Thomas mumbled. "Seems like I'll never kill him. He got me after all."

I did not want to tell him, but I knew I had to.

"It wasn't Isom. *I* shot you."

He seemed to have trouble seeing me clearly. He could not reconcile himself to what I had said. "You're lying. It was Isom."

"It was me. I had to, Thomas. You went crazy."

He shook his head weakly, not accepting.

I said, "If I hadn't, Katy would have. I couldn't let her do that."

Thomas turned his face from me, searching for his daughter. She had not moved. He blinked, trying to bring her to focus.

"Katy . . . you'd have shot me?"

Firmly she said, "I was about to, Papa."

Thomas closed his eyes. He made no sound, but he was weeping.

By this time a dozen cowboys had come running. It took some strong talking on my part and Katy's to keep them from killing the two Isoms on the spot. They listened to Katy more than they listened to me. They had to, for they saw her eyes, the fierce eyes of Thomas Canfield.

The Fernandez brothers fetched a team and wagon. We managed to clot the blood with flour and bind Thomas up enough to hold him. I was lying when I assured Laura that he was going to live. At the time, I did not really believe it. But after Marco and Juan lifted him onto the blankets in the wagon bed and we started for town with him, I began to hope. Laura knelt beside him, oblivious to the bouncing of the vehicle on the rough road. "Hold on, Thomas," she pleaded. "Please don't leave me."

I had not heard her call him anything but "Mr. Canfield" in years.

Katy remained with James and his father. Branch was having trouble standing without support. The last thing I heard him say as we left was to his son and Katy: "You crazy kids. The whole world to choose from, and you had to pick one another."

The doctor said later that if it had taken us much longer to get Thomas to town, he would not have lived. Even as it was, he would suffer from a bad shoulder for however many more years the Lord saw fit to allow him.

I waited on the doctor's porch until Laura came out, weary and red-eyed, to tell me he was awake. She went in with me and sat in the cane-bottomed straight-chair where she had been from the first.

Thomas was pale and sick at his stomach from the chloroform, but his eyes locked on me with a challenge.

"I suppose you've come to apologize," he said.

"No," I told him.

He was disappointed. "You still think I was wrong."

"If I hadn't thought so, I wouldn't have shot you."

He chewed on that awhile, not liking it. "That wasn't a lie, about Katy fixing to shoot me?"

"She was about to. I couldn't let her do that, Thomas. I

couldn't let her live the rest of her life knowing she had killed her own father."

"But *you* could live with it?"

"Yes. We used to be friends, Thomas. But I could have done it." I watched the hurt crowd into his eyes. I added, "Lucky for you I never was much of a shot."

He lay silent awhile. "Have you seen Katy?"

I hated to tell him. "She and James went over to New Silesia. They're talking to the priest about marrying them." I waited a minute before I told him the rest of it. "They asked me to stand up for them. I said I would."

Tears started in Thomas' eyes. "She didn't even come to see me."

"She was here. She stayed until she knew you were going to be all right. That's something, at least."

He closed his eyes. "The bitterest thing of all is to know she would have killed me for that boy . . . an *Isom*."

"He's a good boy, Thomas, better than you or me. You'll see that, someday."

"Isom." He spoke the name as if it were a curse. It *had* been, for much of his life. Acceptance would take time, a lot of time, for "give" was not in Thomas' nature. But ultimately he would have no choice. I suppose he realized that too, because somehow he seemed an old man, vulnerable, dependent.

He said with more despair than hope, "Katy'll come back to me, someday."

I told him, "She's got a Canfield stubbornness about her. You'll have to bend."

Dying would probably be easier. I could only hope he had it in him to bend.

I got up to go. He called for me to stay. I told him I had business of my own to look after.

He pleaded, "I wish you wouldn't, Reed. With Katy gone, and you gone, who have I got left?"

Laura sat staring at him, biting her lip to keep from speaking. A prayer was in her eyes. Up to that minute, I guess I had always hoped there might someday be a chance for me in her life.

I said, "Open your eyes, Thomas. God knows you don't deserve her—you never did—but you've always had somebody."

She reached out to him. He turned his head and looked at her a long time, then slowly raised his hand to hers.

I left them there together and walked out onto the porch, trying to blink away the blurring as the sun hit me in the eyes.

KELTON
ON
KELTON

I was born at a place called Horse Camp on the Scharbauer Cattle Company's Five Wells Ranch in Andrews County, Texas, in 1926. My father was a cowboy there, and my grandfather was the ranch foreman. My great-grandfather had come out from East Texas about 1876 with a wagon and a string of horses to become a ranchman, but he died young, leaving four small boys to grow up as cowpunchers and bronc breakers. With all that heritage I should have become a good cowboy myself, but somehow I never did, so I decided if I could not do it I would write about it.

I studied journalism at the University of Texas and became a livestock and farm reporter in San Angelo, Texas, writing fiction as a sideline to newspaper work. I have maintained the two careers in parallel more than thirty years. My fiction has been mostly about Texas, about areas whose history and people I know from long study and long personal acquaintance. I have always believed we can learn much about ourselves by studying our history, for we are the products of all that has gone before us. All history is relevant today, because the way we live—the values we believe in—are a result of molds prepared for us by our forebears a long time ago.

I was an infantryman in World War II and married an Austrian girl, Anna, I met there shortly after the war. We raised three children, all grown now and independent, proud of their mixed heritage of the Old World on one hand and the Texas frontier on the other.

CARRY THE WIND

By

Terry C. Johnston

Josiah Paddock is a man on the run. He has killed a wealthy young Frenchman in a duel and his flight brings him to the beautiful yet fierce Rocky Mountains in the year 1831. Just as the harshness of mountain life is about to break him, he encounters Titus Bass, a solitary mountain man who teaches him how to survive.

"First-rate entertainment in the steel-trap, 'man's adventure' tradition."
—*Kirkus Reviews*

"This impressive first novel vividly conveys the day-to-day life of a grizzled mountain man ... The effect is one of richness."
—*Publishers Weekly*

"Marked by brutal violence, enduring love, and a passion for the mountains, this is a book worth reading and an author worth watching."
—*Library Journal*

CARRY THE WIND
Coming soon from Bantam Books

BANTAM'S #1
ALL-TIME BESTSELLING AUTHOR
AMERICA'S FAVORITE FRONTIER WRITER

☐ 25206	HELLER WITH A GUN	$2.95
☐ 24550	BOWDRIE'S LAW	$2.95
☐ 23368	BOWDRIE	$2.95
☐ 25100	CROSS FIRE TRAIL	$2.95
☐ 25402	SHOWDOWN AT YELLOW BUTTE	$2.95
☐ 25580	CHANCY	$2.95
☐ 24289	SITKA	$2.95
☐ 20846	THE CHEROKEE TRAIL	$2.95
☐ 25090	MOUNTAIN VALLEY WAR	$2.95
☐ 25477	TAGGART	$2.95
☐ 25972	HIGH LONESOME	$2.95
☐ 25030	BORDEN CHANTRY	$2.95
☐ 24957	BRIONNE	$2.95
☐ 25303	THE FERGUSON RIFLE	$2.95
☐ 25742	KILLOE	$2.95
☐ 25770	CONAGHER	$2.95
☐ 25973	NORTH TO THE RAILS	$2.95
☐ 24906	THE MAN FROM SKIBBEREEN	$2.95
☐ 24743	SILVER CANYON	$2.95
☐ 24767	CATLOW	$2.95
☐ 24765	GUNS OF THE TIMBERLANDS	$2.95
☐ 24762	HANGING WOMAN CREEK	$2.95
☐ 22636	FALLON	$2.50
☐ 24760	UNDER THE SWEETWATER RIM	$2.95
☐ 25221	MATAGORDA	$2.95
☐ 25324	DARK CANYON	$2.95
☐ 20956	THE CALIFORNIOS	$2.50

Prices and availability subject to change without notice.

Buy them at your local bookstore or use this handy coupon:

Bantam Books, Inc., Dept. LL1, 414 East Golf Road, Des Plaines, Ill. 60016

Please send me the books I have checked above. I am enclosing $_____
(please add $1.50 to cover postage and handling). Send check or money order
—no cash or C.O.D.'s please.

Mr/Mrs/Miss_____

Address_____

City_____ State/Zip_____

LL1—3/86

Please allow four to six weeks for delivery. This offer expires 9/86